INTRODUCTION

In the days before written history, clues to everyday events can be found of the existence of a chariot-based civilization in the Western Plains of Russia and Mongolia. This civilization had apparently covered much of the Asian and Chinese as well as the Russian Western Plains.

It was a pre-Celtic way of life. We do not know the names of the tribes or what language they spoke. How did a pre-Viking and pre-Celtic civilization develop into the later domination of the Vikings which was spread throughout Eastern Europe and Western Asia and Russia? Obviously, pre-Gaelic and pre-Viking legends and myth need to be consulted. The longboats of war as well as chariots play a powerful part in these adventures. In those days warrior queens as well as heroic Vikings played a large part.

The latter-day wars organized by Queen Boadicea of Britain who drove the Romans out of the British Isles; Queen Maeve of Connaught who led the united armies of Ireland against Ulster were similarly heroic figures. These warrior queens were fieldmarshals and planners of war as well as chariot warriors. Perhaps the last of this line was Saint Joan of Arc. A statue of Queen Boadicea or Boudicca in her chariot still stands at Westminster Bridge in London.

This tale is based on legends and myths surrounding the warqueens of the past.

LIFE OF DREW CARSON

Sam Drew Carson was born in the North of Ireland and educated there at Wellington College and the Ulster Polytechnic. He completed his education in the USA at New Mexico Highlands University and the University of Arkansas and has traveled widely in North America, around the Atlantic and in Europe.

Drew worked as a seaman and fish-gutter in Vestmannaeyjar off the coast of Iceland. He lived and worked in the Irish and Western Isles Gaeltachts and was married in Welsh-speaking Carmarthen after which he honeymooned in Belfast. He has told his stories, composed and sung his songs, seeking storylines in Bristol and the English Westcountry. Drew has also lived and written in Nashville, Tennessee, in the wooded hills of Mid-America and from the Appalachians to the Ozarks. This was the culture that gave rise to the now worldwide Scotch-Irish country music.

In the USA, he also worked beside the bayous of the French-speaking Cajuns in the South and among the Western Spanish-speaking Navajos, Apaches and Pueblos of the Sangre de Cristo Mountains in New Mexico.

Drew has sailed far into the seas of old Gaelic and Oriental legend. After many years searching for inspiration for story and music, the author is still traveling and writing.

BOOKS BY THE SAME AUTHOR

ZENISUB
Fun and Games in Businezz
ISBN: 978-0-9561435-2-5
GOOD FOR A LAUGH
Six Funny Playscripts for Amateurs
ISBN: 978-0-9561435-3-2
HOME WITH A GOOD COMPANION
Amateur Pantomime Scripts for a Merry Winter
ISBN: 978-0-9561435-4-9
CLASSIC EUROPEAN LYRICS
Translated from the Gaelic, the French and Spanish
ISBN: 978-0-9561435-6-3
COMMONWEALTH
An Introduction to Business Economics
ISBN: 978-0-9561435-7-0
WEREWOLF MURDERS
Detective Felix O'Neill in a Crime Adventure
ISBN: 978-0-9561435-9-4
ORIENTAL GOVERNESS
Detective Felix O'Neill in a Crime Adventure
ISBN: 978-1-908184-00-9
WALLWAVE THE YOUNG SEA WARRIOR
Adventures of War Queens and Battle Heroes
ISBN: 978-1-908184-03-0
WALLWAVE THE SEA PRINCE
Adventures of War Queens and Battle Heroes
ISBN: 978-1-908184-04-7
WALLWAVE THE SEA KING
Adventures of War Queens and Battle Heroes
ISBN: 978-1-908184-05-4
THAT SILVER SHORE
Easter Musical with Ten Songs
ISBN: 978-1-908184-06-1
THE OTHER SIDE
Halloween Masque of Demons and Delusions
ISBN: 978-1-908184-07-8

SEE YOU AROUND
Pantomime of Bygone Fun and Frolic
ISBN: 978-1-908184-08-5
CULT OF THE WIDOW VIDOVA
Detective Felix O'Neill in a Crime Adventure
ISBN: 978-1-908184-09-2
WHITE ZOMBIES OF NEW CASTILE
A Sci-Fi Adventure
ISBN: 978-1-908184-10-8
EASTER AND SPRINGTIME
Six Playscripts about New Life
ISBN: 978-1-908184-12-2

BRITANIA
WarQueen of the Seagulls

by
Drew Carson

Legals

Published by S. A. Carson,
29 Northleaze, Long Ashton, Bristol BS41 9HS, UK
Publisher's email: verygoodreading@googlemail.com

ISBN: 978-1-908184-13-9

CONTENTS

Prologue

PROLOGUE

Who is the tyrant of seas, hills and plains? Who is the sovereign of the air and clouds? Black Weather is the tyrant of the world - brutal and vicious, screaming and unruly, setting up savage storms on the sea of greenweed and undulating hills of swirling foam.

At one time Weather delegated its turmoil into the strength of two great stallions - a Bay and a White - to jointly rule the earth, its men and armies. These two great stallions were given power like two fieldmarshals over their herds to rule and lead wild horses on the moors.

The White, Oceanhorse, the Great White Stallion of the East, was the stallion of the waves born out of the sea storms of the ice.

The Bay, Foresthorse, the Great Bay Stallion of the West, was the leader of the hills, being born out of the steaming jungles and forests.

These horses had the powerful intellect almost of men, especially in ways of war. They were adept at rounding up wild horses and driving them into their combat camps.

Only a horse has all the qualities that go to make up true nobility. It is gentle, sensitive, strong, proud and delicate yet difficult to master or subdue.

A stallion is an earl, a viceking, an admiral of the moors. Only man is the master of the horse - no other animal could stand before it.

The horse is not a crude machine of battle. It has great dignity and decency of spirit and is not petty minded or quick to change. It is a true noble surrounded by long knives lurking to kill.

All the great warriors of old rode on a horse. Many of the great fieldmarshals of war rode on a horse or posed astride its back - proud to be seen in charge and in the saddle. For the horse imparts its own nobility and its own calm control to the horserider. The hero is the man or woman on the white horse. For true nobility does not come from acclaim or from the approbation of a Vi-King. Rather, nobility surges from within like a wallwave of the inner spirit. All horses have this spirit of nobility but the great stallions of the world have also a splendid gentility and courage.

These were the qualities seen in the White, Oceanhorse of the East and the Great Bay Stallion, Foresthorse of the West.

* * *

MAIN CHARACTERS IN THIS TALE

SEAGULL WAVEWARRIORS
Waterbear, King of the Seagull Wavewarriors
Springvision, Queen
Britania, WarQueen of the Seagulls
Stormbolt, younger brother of Britania
Summersailor, fieldmarshal and brother of Waterbear
Whaleroarer, fieldmarshal
Stormleaper, fieldmarshal
Icedragon, fieldmarshal
Seaspear, admiral

EAGLE WARRIORS
Warchariot, King of the Eagle Warriors
Snakeknife, WarQueen
Sternrider, fieldmarshal
Winterwarrior, fieldmarshal and future king
Winterfire, son of Winterwarrior

THE IMMORTALS
Four Witches
Mooncrow
Truthteller

CHAPTER ONE

The Coming of Britania

Waterbear, King of the Wavewarriors was a tall and noble king with the light of justice shining on his face. His silver hair was curly, kingly and imperial. The grim glint of a protector of his people shone from his grey-blue eyes and his eyebrows bristled of black and grey and white across his forehead.

One day Waterbear opened his castle that stood beside a harbor of the ocean for a three day festival of the sea where the Wavewarriors tested their skills of fishing, hunting and warfare. They spent time recounting boasts of their past combats, displaying mock battles and tricks of fighting. Then they took out their hunting dogs to find and fetch small game and birds. The leader of the dog pack was Guardhunt, a loyal and good-natured dog that all the other dogs feared and respected for his great strength and speed and sense of smell. Guardhunt belonged to Whaleroarer, one of the four fieldmarshals of the Wavewarriors.

On the third day they rode into the hills to hunt for deer with the dogs being led by Guardhunt when suddenly a beautiful roe appeared before them. Immediately their pack of dogs rushed forward and began to frolic and fawn around the roe.

The warriors were astounded to see that Guardhunt made no attempt to kill or cower the roe but rather made a friend of it. The other dogs took their cue from the pack leader and loped around and bowed and licked in fun. The roe turned sharply from the beaten track and headed straight for the castle of Waterbear followed by the playful Guardhunt. The dogs escorted the roe into the castle all closely followed by the Seagull Warriors while the hunting troop continued with their pursuit of other game.

Waterbear remarked to Whaleroarer that he couldn't understand why Guardhunt was so friendly and protective. However, the roe would still be inside the castle keep when they got back.

The Wavewarriors continued with the hunt and later, at the end of the day, they returned home with salmon and wild boar for their festival. When they sat down to feast at the open fire in the courtyard of the castle of Waterbear there was no sign of any roe or deer. The warriors sang the songs of old and told their stories and drank toasts of wine to their sea heroes.

Later in the evening Waterbear walked across the courtyard to the well and the bright fountain that sprang out of the ground, a waterspring of the sun that glittered and gleamed in the pale moonlight. Suddenly there stood before him a young and beautiful woman whom he had never seen before.

The stunned Waterbear asked her, "Who are you?"

She replied, "I am the roe that your dogs escorted here earlier in the day. Where is Guardhunt?"

And Waterbear replied to the strange young girl, "No doubt he is over in the Whaleroarer camp whose dog he is but why have you come here?"

As she answered him, Waterbear saw that her hair was black and thick and loose for washing and her skin was yellow golden like the dawn. She held in her hands a gold and silver comb with a silver basin decorated with bluebirds and colored gems set all around the rim. The moonlight shone on her yellow shoulders above a bodice of blue silk as she prepared to wash her hair in the silver bowl. Her long white skirt was laced with golden fringes and blue-gold brooches shone at her silken neck.

Her eyes were brown as the sunflower in the summer – a brown bulb surrounded by bright yellow leaves when the bees fly round and buzz in the hazy air. Her lips were as red as rowanberries in springtime and her teeth as white as the bright foam of the wave. The yellow light of the moon was on her face as her dark eyebrows rose like thin black arches.

The voice of the young woman was like soft bells of waterfalls in a cave of tinkling waters and rainbows. Her step was full of grace and elegance, even and balanced and like a dancing queen. Around her was an aura of flowers and trees – a faint aroma of blue days in woodlands. All ladies of high birth are beautiful until you see the beauty of Springvision. It was as though she sprang out of a sea of tropical green grasses and brown corals shining and shimmering in a pool of sunlight.

"I am Springvision, a princess of the orient," she told Waterbear. "The old witch Meteoreyes once envied me my youth and wanted me to enter a trance where she would invade my mind and memory. She planned to possess and hold my spirit and my mind and use my beauty to ensnare young kings and princes.

"When I refused her promises, the four witches of kill gathered around. Meteoreyes put a long spell on me and changed me into the roe that Guardhunt guided here today. The spell worked for everywhere except the royal sovereign. For it was not permitted by the powers of good for the witches to take over the kingdoms of the world. So that is why I took flight and fled the woods to the safety of your castle."

"You are a vision beside a spring of beauty so I will call you now and forever Springvision," Waterbear told her.

All around them shone a purple aura covering the well and spring. Wild boar, salmon, cups and plates appeared beside the water from the hillside fountain.

Suddenly, a tall thin grey-haired man dressed in the plain clothes of a wandering student stood before them and spoke to King Waterbear and Springvision, "Eat and drink here within this pure purple aura. This water comes from a bright and pleasant hillside."

Springvision was thirsty and she drank long and deep with a large helping from the silver salmon. Waterbear ate just a little salmon and a large piece of boar, drinking it down with many cups of the water.

All the food and drink gleamed in the purple glow but after they had eaten the aura died and the food and water returned to its former color.

The grey-haired man said, "I am the Truthteller and I have enchanted all this food and water to celebrate your coming marriage and the warriors who will come after. I will guide your lives but only as you have eaten of this food and drunk the water in the purple glow. It was your choice. That was the boar of courage, speed and strength in battle and that was the salmon of wisdom and the water was the crystal stream of truth and honor."

"If only we had known this," cried Waterbear.

And Truthteller replied in his keen wisdom, "We cannot all have courage, skill and honor in equal measures. Such is the wheel of fortune – it must spin uniquely for each person. Only your daughter, Britania, to be known as WarQueen Britania, will have all the attributes of a great hero. For she will show courage, skill and honor in battle."

Then the Truthteller stepped into the fountain spring and disappeared from the eyes of the young couple.

Later Waterbear and Springvision were married and lived in their castle and outer courtyard. For seven years Springvision did not leave the castle for fear that the spell of metamorphoses of the witches should again transform her. During this time Waterbear stood beside her to protect her from the spells and potions of the envious witch.

But at the end of seven years, Eagle Warriors sailed in scrappy boats as cutthroat pirates and invaded the islands of the Wavewarriors. They plundered and pillaged all the Seagull people. So Waterbear had to leave his castle to pursue the invaders. He gathered together his warriors and ships and bade a tender farewell to Springvision.

King Waterbear warned her never to leave the palace walls for he feared that the spell of Meteoreyes would seize Springvision and change her once again into a roe. She promised never to leave the castle until he returned.

As Waterbear sailed away, Springvision waved from the rampart of the castle then he cried out to remind her, "Take care Springvision. Do not step outside our castle courtyard or speak to a stranger and when I come back we will be happy once more."

Waterbear pushed hard against the Eagle pirates, wrecking and burning their ships but they fought hard and every inch of ocean foam was bought with Seagull blood. At last the pirates were left dead or floating with scraps of wood and ropes and sails choking them as they cried out in the green seaweed.

As Waterbear and his Wavewarriors sailed back home with his hands still dripping wet with red blood from the bitter combat, he thought only of the warm reunion with his beloved Springvision.

The ship of Waterbear cut through the waves approaching his castle that shone in the sunlight. But he saw no glimpse or glimmer, no handwaving or scarf flying high in the sky to welcome him back home. Nor was there any face in any window. And when the longboat of Waterbear sailed into his wide harbor all the servants avoided his firm gaze. They looked away in solemn silence and uneasy quietness as though they were glancing sideways at the king.

Brave Waterbear shivered and felt a lump, a stone, sinking far down inside his stomach.

Then he asked his servants, "Where is Queen Springvision? Why does she not come to meet me?"

An older servant turned to Waterbear and looked him in the eye, "The Queen Springvision is gone, brave Waterbear. One day a figure that looked like you appeared outside the courtyard. There was a dog that looked like our Guardhunt with other dogs and a chariot nearby. We saw a shade or shape that looked like Waterbear cry out in pain as though he had been stabbed. He walked like one who had been wounded, limped slowly towards the gate and then shouted out, please help us Springvision, Guardhunt and I are both injured. Help me, my Queen.

"We urged Springvision not to go. We pleaded that we should be allowed to help for we suspected that it was a sameshape conjured from the pit. But Springvision ran to the darkling figure outside the gates. As she came close to it we saw the vague shape shimmer in the sun and realized it was not Waterbear nor was the dog Guardhunt. It snarled and growled. Springvision screamed and shrank back but it was too late for she had changed back into a red roe and the false dog swiftly chased her into the woods.

"We seized our weapons and pursued the roe and the chariot. We followed the sounds of horses and barking of dogs but they had fled deep into the woods. Springvision had been so quick in dashing out that she had disappeared from sight in a few seconds. We have felt guilt and terror ever since."

But Waterbear told his servants, "Feel neither guilt nor terror for it is my responsibility to find her and break the spell and bring her home again."

Then brave Waterbear went to visit Whitehair, the young niece of Summersailor. Only a child, she had the gift of foresight and discernment of spirits. She told Waterbear, "When the seas recoil and whip into high waves, go to the ocean-side and call aloud to Springvision. Then, winds will roar and carry abroad your call and when she hears, your queen will do the rest."

So Waterbear went back to his own room above the sea and waited for the storm. For three days and three nights he did not eat but prayed to the powers of good in the universe. Then on a nearby island the earth shook and lava poured out from the fiery hilltop as waves leapt up and clawed in the fierce wind.

Realizing that the four elements were in harmony in a deep and ominous and auspicious way, Waterbear took his hawk and hounds and sailed on the rough seas among the little islands and called aloud, "Springvision, we have come to find you."

The moon began to fade in the dawn light and soon the sun arose upon the red ocean, sending its rays along the choppy waves. Guardhunt leapt up and whined and moaned and barked as he left the boat and swam to a small island.

Waterbear steered his ship after Guardhunt and there he found Springvision in a pool of corals, flowers and leaves. Swimming beside her was a young girl, whose skin glowed with brightness, floating among the lilies.

Waterbear acclaimed the stormchild as his own and named her Brightania as a future warqueen of the Wavewarriors. She was yellow-skinned and oriental with dark hair and brown eyes like sunflowers set in a gold ring of yellow leaves just like her mother, Springvision. She was strong and active in the pools and waves.

The deep wallwave of the seas recoiling, the earth turmoiling, lava and flames arising and the loud roar of thunder cracking the island had smashed apart the spell of the four witches and set Springvision free to return home.

Even at an early age Brightania broke the weapons that children play with and then begged Waterbear to give her the weapons of a fully grown warrior. When attacked by a wolf she speared it to death. She later strangled a young bear and stabbed a shark to death under the water.

As was the custom, Brightania was sent to foster with a farming family who fished and sailed and fought as foot soldiers. Their name was Kim and they loved her dearly. Brightania's great-uncle Shadowhero was an older man retired from active war. He set about training her in all the feats of combat and hard fighting.

In her early life she won the magic Shield of Roar that warns of danger. It was presented to her by the popular acclaim of Seagull heroes, sitting in council on the rules of warfare. Its orle fringe quivers when it hears the sound of coming danger and lets out a roar of warning to its owner. The young warqueen also won the Bonespear that thirsts for blood and never fails to crunch bone and the Rainbow-Hardblade sword that paints a rainbow in the sky when it is whirled high in the air by any warrior.

As the years went by, King Waterbear thought about these things and asked himself what could young Brightania be capable of when fully grown?

*****

CHAPTER TWO
Murder of a King

For many years Waterbear, King of the Wavewarriors, continued to rule his eastern kingdom with his Queen Springvision and their four fieldmarshals: Summersailor - his brother, Whaleroarer, Icedragon and Stormleaper.

It appeared that the Wavewarriors were no longer being threatened by their enemies the Eagle Warriors led by their King Warchariot and his WarQueen Snakeknife who was in the habit of consulting the four witches of kill and the Mooncrow.

But once again the Eagles became restless and revived the old jealousies and ambitions so that they began to make plots against Waterbear.

King Warchariot was a giant warrior with thick black hair and beard as smooth as silk. His eyes were grey and his savage teeth were sparkling and bright flashing out from thick lips of blackberry and red. His brows were brooding over his piercing eyes like two great shaggy bears in a black forest.

WarQueen Snakeknife was slender and tall. Her hair was long and red and flowing wild, held back in place with a gold band on her forehead to stop the hair from falling over her dark eyes. Behind her ears were two broad rings of gold and into these her red hair had been gathered.

So when King Warchariot and his Queen, the warriorwoman, Snakeknife, went again to seek wisdom of war they dressed in their full regalia of combat as they rode in their battle chariots to consult with the witches.

The four witches of kill lived with the Mooncrow in their castle where they lured away the unwary traveler by spells and visions. The witches crawled in their lair deep among cobwebs – the place of spiders.

Windweasel clutched the air with her sharp wrinkled claws and sneered with her toothless mouth.

Meteroeyes had eyes that looked like burning flames. Her head was as bald as stone and her warted mouth twisted tightly closed.

Landslink was a wrinkled, wizened and gaunt old crone with blackened sharp teeth like burnt-out embers.

Rivershark was a daughter of the tomb, now kept alive only by spells and potions that stoked the flames of life in the living dead.

King Warchariot and his WarQueen Snakeknife bowed low and asked the witches, "We are plagued by the presence of Wavewarriors, fierce men in ships, who come to kill and plunder. The time has come to drive these eastern pirates back into the sea. Is it auspicious, on this dull day, to launch a just warstab to protect those who pay their tax to us?"

The witches of kill consulted among themselves, "We have powers to help you whether the time is right or no. Let us now call upon the spirits of war and ask for their advice. We call upon the Mooncrow who is mistress of all battles."

Then Mooncrow, cawed on a rafter of the witches' lair, flew down and slowly changed its form into an old and wizened hag, her skin grown gray with age and grizzled like seal leather and her thin hooked nose as vicious as an eagle.

As the Mooncrow stood erect, the lightning flashed and moonbeams lit the air. Low thunder rattled and rain fell.

The Mooncrow pointed to the clouds of darkened blood gathering over the castle. "That is the most red sunset I have ever seen, good for shepherds no doubt but surely a sign of doom, death and destruction for you and your Eagle Warriors."

WarQueen Snakeknife sneered. She was dressed as a warriorwoman decked for battle with shield, sword, javelins and daggers around her waist. Spiked wolf-heads hung on chains upon her wrists. She was taller than anyone else in the dark room.

She held high her head and laughed defiantly, a queenly and a haughty and a warlike laugh. Then looking down upon the Mooncrow and the witches she said, "That sunset is far at sea, no doubt it bodes ill with its blood clouds for seamen and for the Seagulls and all Wavewarriors."

The four witches eagerly nodded their assent to WarQueen Snakeknife.

The Mooncrow was not pleased and changed back into a bird and flew up high, once more into the rafters cawing and crying, "The sign of destruction for you and your Eagle Warriors."

Both Snakeknife and Warchariot stood like warriors struck dumb who had not understood a word nor cared, for they had come to seek success for war and nothing else was of any interest to them.

Then Warchariot again asked the witches, "What shall we do now about the Seagulls coming here and how can we drive them away?"

And Snakeknife spoke up, "How can we avoid a warhost invading us like a plague of hungry Seagulls? For very soon Britania, the young daughter of Waterbear, will come and pour out her anger on our chariot warriors. Soon to stand up beside her will be her younger brother Stormbolt. We outnumber them but they have skills of combat and tricks of war-trade to help them win."

Windweasel answered, "Therefore you must kill their leader."

Meteoreyes agreed, "Your armies are made up of too many factions. Those who fight reluctantly and out of fear and those who believe the tax that they have paid you should buy them relief from going to war.

"In the same way the Seagulls must be split up. You must divide the Wavewarriors for they are now united in the brotherhood of the sea."

Then Landslink reminded them, "King Warchariot, you are the step-brother of the Seagull King, brave Waterbear. You must use your family knowledge and your understanding to catch him unawares and kill him then the Seagulls will surely fight over who should succeed Waterbear."

Windweasel agreed, "Britania will soon become their greatest champion when she is ready to take over. As for the younger son, Stormbolt, leave him to us for we have magic powers and spells to tame him.

"Consider their present King, old Waterbear, if mangy, miserable dogs can drive the cunning and wily fox far from his lair, then surely you and the tall Queen Snakeknife can contrive to bring great Waterbear to his downfall, a place where he can be assassinated."

Warchariot shook his head, "He does not trust me. I am only his step-brother. He would not enter any trap I set for him. Indeed I would be lucky if he would come even to my funeral and that would not help me nor help you."

Meteoreyes spoke up, "Indeed it might help us if you were still alive and waiting for him."

WarQueen Snakeknife lit up, "I see it now, a false funeral and a request to come and make peace and let bygones be bygones. A trap is set and Waterbear is caught."

Landslink agreed, "There is an ancient burial ceremony reserved for mighty warriors like you Warchariot. In those past days a king who died was kept lying in state in his own chariot, surrounded by his swords and spears and daggers, to be buried in a swamp and so preserved for all time in an underworld of honor. Let such a burial be yours Warchariot but let the staring eyes of the dead man be wary of who approaches him. Your faithful Queen Snakeknife will usher in the mourners of your death, including Waterbear, the King of Seagulls."

Then Meteoreyes spoke up, "King Warchariot, we will proclaim your death as the passing of a hero worthy of burial in a chariot of war like the ancient kings. King Waterbear will hear of this and will be likely to make peace with Snakeknife the weeping widow but you Warchariot will be more alive than ever you have been."

Rivershark finally explained to the Snakeknife and to the King Warchariot, "Remember, the Seagulls set their dead heroes in a ship and steer it to the West. Set it on fire to be sure that it passes to the other world, so they will understand your noble burial."

Then Warchariot went home and hid deep in his castle while his wife, Queen Snakeknife proclaimed his death to all.

***

Now King Waterbear and his brother Summersailor walked by the ramparts of their castle and looked out to the sea that separated the Wavewarriors, those Seagulls of the sun, from their enemy the Eagles of the West.

Then Summersailor pointed to the sky beyond the swirling mist, "See, where that smoke arises there is death and burntout bones and homes and a large black bird rises and flies across the sky."

"Death it is certain," agreed King Waterbear, "but perhaps that smoke is not really speaking of war. Our Seagulls would certainly have warned us of destruction or any burnings or murders or mayhem. It may be just the formal burial of a warrior. It looks to be a symbol."

As they spoke, a green and yellow bird with fine and shining feathers circled above in the sunlight and flew slowly around flapping its wings. Then it settled with its gripping claws upon the parapet of the fastness, where it stood screeching aloud, "Come, come and see the dead."

Then the bird transformed into a woman messenger of beauty with yellow hair that flowed down upon her robes of bright green that lay around her claws.

Her sharp, black eyes stared at King Waterbear, "King Warchariot is dead and lies in state in the stone tomb below his fortress. There he sits in full accoutrements of war, a hero in his chariot evermore. Soon he will be buried and preserved in a great swamp as a memorial, just like the mighty chariotkings of old.

"Go now and mourn the passing of Warchariot, your fellow king and almost a kind of brother to you once. Go and comfort his widow who is alone and childless and perhaps the Eagle Warriors might seek you as their king of a united people.

"Enter your longboat and swiftly sail away to talk of peace. The cautious Eagles would never permit a fleet to enter in upon them for fear they might be hacked with swords and enslaved by their old foes. But if you come alone, clearly in peace, perhaps this will unite our warring peoples. Of course, you may go armed for self-defense with a small troop."

The bird of message laughed and spread her claws and shook her arms like wings and flew away.

Then Queen Springvision came out into the sunlight from the shadows, "I saw and heard it all," she said. "The wind is cold. Let us go down below and talk about this message from a bird and consider what is behind this omen."

In the great sunroom of the palace, Queen Springvision spoke to Waterbear and to his brother Summersailor who was second in the kingdom. "They will never let you approach with a large force sufficient for your protection. They have said so, because they fear you. Why should they so fear if they would seriously consider you for their king? What nonsense! It is a snap-trap. Do not go. If you are killed, all mayhem will break loose."

"Calm down my dear wife," replied Waterbear, "This duty brings honor to my own rank as a king. Although at enmity with him while still alive, death is the door that opens up new visions. Also, my dear wife, there is no one among the Eagle Warriors who is strong enough to frame a plot against me.

"Now that the chariot king is dead and gone my step-brother's warriors will be in a state of chaos and fighting each other for the throne. Who knows, perhaps I can become kingmaker if not the king and broker the cause of someone friendly to us. And do not fear that I seek a second wife, for I have no such need. You have been all that I have ever loved, my wife, Queen Springvision."

"I know, I worry for your life not your devotion. Is it to be for peace or enmity within their gates - who knows? So take no risks for the sly WarQueen Snakeknife is still alive and well."

And Summersailor agreed, "Yes, stay with us. There is no need to go and mourn with Snakeknife."

Then seeing that their warnings were of no avail, Springvision went away and looked out over the dark sea and wept.

Waterbear turned to his younger brother Summersailor, "My brother, I am mid-aged and soon must die in any case. If I do not return I leave my kingdom to the young WarQueen Britania when she is ready. In that way you will be the uncle of a warriorqueen."

And Summersailor agreed, "Just so, my brother. This is agreed. I will look forward to her reign one day. But today, I still swear my allegiance to you and yours, great Waterbear. My blood is yours to spill and

yet we must be careful. Our mighty ships
and our great Hawkarmy, the crack division,
pride of all our troops, are scattered and
need food and weaponry."

And Waterbear replied, "Take the
command of the whole crack division,
known as the Hawkarmy. While I am gone
away upon this mission I appoint you to be
their fieldmarshal for life if I should not
return to take my place. But then all is not
yet lost, for I will return I do believe and
take back the command and so demote you."

Summersailor smiled, "May it be so,"
he said and they shook hands as the sun
sank silently behind a cloud.

Brave Waterbear put on his battle
armor, his sword and shield and spear and
axe and dagger and all his other
accoutrements of combat. Then he called
Springvision to his side and kissed her,
saying, "Farewell, but just for now, for I am
confident that I will return and you will see
me standing in my ship, sailing into this
harbor in the mists. I will come home once
more with duty done."

And Springvision put her head upon his shoulder and warned him once more to beware of the sly Queen Snakeknife.

Then the king called to his side his close attendants and set sail in his longboat for the burial ceremony. As the stately rowers gently steered the boat out of the harbor, there suddenly appeared upon the shore the figure of an old washerwoman. She was dressed in red robes, her face shriveled and ugly, wailing and weeping as she washed her clothes and pounded them upon the redstained rocks. The rowers paused and all looked at the woman as she wrung red blood from every sheet and garment, red flowing away from her like a river of slaughter.

"What do you see, old woman?" asked King Waterbear, "Whose garments do you wash?" he asked her.

"I wash your clothes. I wash your vest of wool. See the white wool as cool as mountain snow; see how it flows away from me in blood. I rinse white shirts in water clear as crystal and it flows away from me as a river of thick and bubbling living blood, hot to the touch."

"What of the young Princess Britania, you seer?" asked Waterbear.

"Britania will win many battles above all your foes," the old hag replied, "Turn back; it is not too late to flee your fate."

Then the vision of the prophetess grew vague and hazy and disappeared into the misty air.

As Waterbear watched her go, he told his men, "Vague prophecies mean little. What if I sow wild seeds of victory in the blood of others? She sees the coming victories for Britania to reap.

"Yet, all vile witches are on the side of the Eagles. It has been known for a long time that witches are plotting devious and scheming plans to make sure that the Seagulls are driven out, while the Eagles take up the lordship of all lands. Why would they want to warn us of defeat or try to help us in anyway at all? If these grim witches warn us not to travel then some great triumph for us must lie ahead. Let us go forward always in peace, I say."

Yet, at this time, Waterbear did not hear the laughter in the air of sniggering witches. Brave Waterbear forged ahead in his longboat, proudly as a hero going to pay his homage to another hero who had died in peace.

Now, far towards the red setting dusk he sailed past many islands. Round about his head the seagulls screamed and the crias sang aloud as falcons swooped like a flying crown of champions around his head.

Then he arrived at the castle of Warchariot. It was surrounded by cruel crocodiles in the moat but soon the drawbridge was lowered to receive him. And Waterbear and his small troop arrived to mourn, with dignity and respect, the death of the Eagle King Warchariot.

The castle of Warchariot appeared to be in mourning with windows darkened by long dismal curtains and the faces of the servants were drawn and dark, for Snakeknife, Queen of Warchariot had announced his death. Yet the mourners and all the nobles and the heroes of the Eagle kingdom were intent on drinking and making merry, laughing and eating with dancers, dwarfs, jugglers and joyful singing. This was a wake that well could have been continued after the death of Waterbear had been achieved. Indeed, it was a feast designed to last for many days after the funeral. But no one, other than the evil WarQueen Snakeknife, knew that King Warchariot lived and laid in wait nearby.

Then servants and attendants were sent to Waterbear and his small group, bringing them music, dancers, strong sweet-scented drinks and savories.

The small group all partook of these enchantments except Waterbear. He stood aloof and waited until the darkcowled Snakeknife approached and bid him welcome to the funeral. She was falsely weeping and sorrowing with her waiting ladies, one on each arm.

Waterbear murmured his respects, "Condolences, I am most sorry Queen Snakeknife."

"Thank you King Waterbear, my husband asked that you should come to mourn and to memorialize his funeral so that our two peoples may be at peace."

Dismissing her attendants, she spoke softly, "Come, I am going to his funeral chariot down these stone steps, to the lying-in-state basement from which he will be borne away for burial in a deep swamp, just like the kings of old."

Then Waterbear, like a true king, upright and dignified, with weapons and his shield still proud upon him, followed the grieving widow dressed in her flowing, darkest weeds and veils, down the steep steps into the pit of peril.

Down in the stone room of lying in state, Warchariot sat upright in his chariot in full regalia, like the kings of old. His eyes stared straight ahead. Around the walls, beside the spears and shields for a long battle, were bits and bridles and trappings of two horses and urns of eastern craft for drinking wine.

Warchariot's face was painted white and black. He wore all his accoutrements of combat: his silver shoulder pieces and his helmet; his boots and armlets bright with burnished mail; his belts and buckles for his knives and dirks; his silver helmet with a neckshield of bronze. Set firm along his round brass shield of war, at his left side, were three lances and a sword. In his right hand was a large and shining dagger.

Only three candles burned in the burial chamber. A roar of revelry and making merry and singing could be heard coming from above. The dark-veiled widow knelt beside the body and bowed for prayer to the gods of war.

Waterbear also knelt down beside the false widow and bowed his head as a token of respect.

Suddenly Warchariot raised his dagger and struck deep into the back of the bowed down Waterbear. The blade sank through the cloak and purple tunic till the knifetip showed at the heart of Waterbear who fell in agony and gasped and died.

Suddenly WarQueen Snakeknife tore the dark veils from her face and from her body and threw them to the floor; for underneath she wore a bright silken dress. Screaming with joy, she danced up the tomb steps and joined the dancers and the drinking.

Then Warchariot appeared at the top of the tomb steps holding across his arms the bleeding body of the now dead King Waterbear. The merriment fell silent as horror struck the mourners and the servants as they realized that they had been an unwitting party to such a murder. They stared with fear until the body of Waterbear was taken by his servants to his ship. After the dead Waterbear had gone, the mourners took again to laughing and singing and dancing.

Shocked and mind-blown, like the walking dead, the small stunned troop of Wavewarriors sailed back and bore the body of their leader King Waterbear home to the palace of the Seagull Warriors.

***

So it was that the grieving Queen Springvision placed the body of her dead husband Waterbear in a longboat filled with sword and axe and javelins. She set up Waterbear in his best tunic and in his armor for head and chest and limbs, decked in his full accoutrements of war.

Then the boat and sails and body were set on fire as the rudder was fixed to sail due west as the Wavewarriors sent it sailing to the Isles of Youth.

Unseen by the other mourners, Queen Springvision stole out to a great crag overlooking the burning ship and leapt into it to be with her loved husband on his last journey. And so she perished with him.

*****

CHAPTER THREE
A Wavewarrior joins the Eagles

As the years went by, the memory of the death of King Waterbear grew dim. But once again Warchariot, King of the Eagle Warriors and his WarQueen Snakeknife consulted with the four witches. This time they took along their two fieldmarshals, Sternrider and Winterwarrior for they wanted to know the omens for their planned coming war against the Wavewarriors.

The witches assured them they had omens a-plenty but they also had powers to help them win, whether the time was right or wrong, whether the omens told of a defeat or a great victory.

Landslink told fieldmarshal Sternrider to avoid a bloodbath where most of their best warriors would die, the witches could lure a Seagull of high rank, possibly Seaspear, to change sides and join with the Eagles Warriors. Then they would conjure up beckoning ghosts to lure the four fieldmarshals of the Wavewarriors to the otherworld of dreams.

So the four witches set up their battle plan and stared into the flames to see what images would emerge.

Meteoreyes spoke up, "We need to bring clear visions to each fieldmarshal of the Seagulls in his own fastness far away from any interference from young Britania and the other Wavewarriors.

Windweasel looked into the flames and spoke, "Then, in the absence of their fieldmarshals and heroes, the lands and harbors of the Seagulls can be invaded by your Eagle armies and you can drive away their herds of horses leaving only empty stables and foot soldiers. This will leave a young WarQueen to stand alone against her enemies when her main champions and heroes have gone.

"For you will have seized the horses of the Seagulls leaving them only empty chariots rotting and falling apart and rusting over in the cold, wet, wintry place that they call home."

As they all sat in the dark castle and drank the dark red wine of battle vision and ate the eels of wily cunning schemes, WarQueen Snakeknife also suggested that it would be easy to seize a hostage, perhaps a close friend of Britania, once their four heroes have been taken away to Isles of the Everyoung.

Then the witches laid out their greater strategy, "We also need a Seer of Win to lift the hearts and minds of all your warriors to encourage them and build up the hope of winning. The Queen of Justice is a false teller of omens who can be easily bribed to predict a victory."

Pleased at the words of the witches Warchariot and Snakeknife, along with their two fieldmarshals, returned to their castle of the Eagle Warriors.

At they approached their fastness, a tall young woman stood before their gaze. Her hair was black and her eyes and skin were red. Around her long face hung two soft black tresses and her long black eyelashes cast a shadow upon each cheek, making her face seem broad across the eyes and narrower at the chin. Her lips were like strawberries and her teeth were white and glistening like deep-sea pearls. She wore a flowing cloak of red around her and two shoes with buckles of red gold. Her chariot was drawn by two black horses and all around them was an aura of night.

WarQueen Snakeknife asked the young woman in the black chariot, "My armies are now hosting; will they win?"

"I am the Red Warriorwoman – a seer. I see only a haze of red upon your armies – a fog of misty blood floats over their heads."

Snakeknife continued, "In an assembly of young men and warriors there are bound to be manly fights among them and some will come to blows and shed red blood. Look once again and tell me what you see?"

"I see a mist of red, a crimson fog."

"No," Warchariot cried loudly, "You are mistaken. You do not understand. In a huge hosting like our mighty army, there are bound to be many who will die in triumph and be held in honor. Take a new look at the final outcome. Now, tell me what do you see – success or failure?"

The young woman replied, "I see red blood. I see a mighty warrior from the lakes and snow plains of the East who will destroy your army like a tempest."

Snakeknife was furious and reached for her javelin. "Liar," she screamed.

But Warchariot said, "No, do not bring any bad luck upon us. Let us improve our armies to the point where they will be sure to overwhelm our enemies. We need to get more wisdom from the four witches because they have many schemes and devious magic that will ensure success."

The Red Warriorwoman sneered at Snakeknife and drove off in anger.

"Yes," agreed Snakeknife, "we shall wait until the omens are more favorable.

"Maybe the mathematics of the stars will be more lucky and more auspicious to us after we have talked later to the four witches of kill."

Snakeknife and Warchariot called for singers, storytellers and readers of secret omens but the wise ones were reluctant to foretell bad outcomes and held back the fatal news until a better omen could be found.

Then Snakeknife sent for the woman calling herself the Queen of Justice who asked for a huge amount of gold and silver and promised to examine stars and fortunes in a clear light of favorable omens.

WarQueen Snakeknife spoke to the king, Warchariot, "That sounds just what we need, someone to examine our fortunes in a favorable light rather than listen to these seers who hate us."

However, Warchariot was doubtful of the Queen of Justice but nevertheless agreed to hear her false omens in the hope that many would believe them to be true.

The Queen of Justice looked into a bowl of steaming water then declared her vision. "I see the pale blue sky of victory. I see a haze of blue upon your hosts."

Then Snakeknife welcomed this vision of victory, "Now we can press ahead with the advice of the witches."

So Snakeknife made a hard and solemn promise, "We must now get one of the admirals of the Wavewarriors to join us."

"But we have great heroes too," cried Warchariot, "There is Sternrider who is swift and fearless."

Then remembering the words of the witch known as Landslink the sly Snakeknife replied, "Sternrider is our fieldmarshal, yet I wish to have one of the Wavewarriors for his skill in boats – I mean, of course, Seaspear."

"Then let Seaspear beware of you, Snakeknife," said Warchariot.

"Just so, Warchariot," she replied and laughed loudly.

But Warchariot reminded her that it would not be easy to persuade any Wavewarrior to join them in battle because the Seagulls were proud masters of the sea and they would never wish to split their ranks.

The Queen of Justice reminded the king and queen, "In that case you should vigorously deny to Seaspear and the other Wavewarriors that you have any intention of going into battle against them."

So Snakeknife and Warchariot pledged peace and respect for law to lure Seaspear to their side but in the Eagle camp, WarQueen Snakeknife stood up within her chariot and raised her javelin above her head as she rode all around her Eagle hosts, shouting, "Yes, war. Let us prepare for war."

***

Meanwhile, rumors of these plots and war ambitions drifted over to the camp of the Seagull Warriors and to the castle of Wavewarriors.

Suddenly the Mooncrow appeared before them perched on the rampart. "King Warchariot and his Queen Snakeknife invite you, Seaspear, to a place of honor as admiral of all their fleet. You may remain as an advisor to the Seagulls – no secret plans will be kept from you."

Slowly the Mooncrow changed into a hag and limped around, then turned with a cunning sneer and flew away.

Gentleleaf, the wife of Seaspear, began to plead with him not to accept or he would become the enemy of the Seagull Warriors. Then Summersailor and the three other fieldmarshals took Seaspear aside to discuss the offer made by King Warchariot.

When they had gone Gentleleaf pleaded with the young Britania, "I do not trust

Snakeknife or Warchariot. I would not turn my back on them."

Britania agreed.

But later when the four fieldmarshals of the Wavewarriors sat down to eat and drink together, the spells of the witches of kill began to slowly take hold of their minds.

Then Seaspear spoke up, "I want to have a foot in both our camps, so let us all agree that we will never take the field against each other."

And they all shook hands as a pledge based on their longtime friendship.

Later Gentleleaf again begged her husband, "Be aware Seaspear and know that Warchariot and his sly WarQueen Snakeknife are not to be trusted to walk the paths of peace. They secretly plan and plot for war."

"I know this, Gentleleaf, I have heard these rumors."

But Gentleleaf remained sad with a foreboding. It was as though a cloud had blocked the sunlight that once had shone on the garden of her marriage.

Later, in the camp of the Eagles, Sternrider presided over a council of peace with Winterwarrior, Warchariot and Queen Snakeknife to welcome Seaspear as an admiral.

"Surely this is an omen of success," he told the others.

And when Seaspear arrived Sternrider welcomed him to the castle of Snakeknife and Warchariot. They went to the throne room where they could talk about their plans. The king and queen smiled and shook hands with Seaspear and offered him a glass of wine and they all drank to the success of their mission.

Seaspear raised his glass of the red wine of courage, "May both our peoples work together in peace."

Then King Warchariot spoke to Seaspear, "We know of your four great fieldmarshals, the swiftest and most deadly in the world: the Whaleroarer, Stormleaper, Icedragon and Summersailor."

Snakeknife interrupted, "But who is Britania and what is the strange story of her birth? Is it true that she is one of the Immortals?"

Seaspear replied, "I cannot say for sure because there is great mystery surrounding her origin. She is mortal but her godfather is Truthteller the Immortal with the silver darts of truth who wears the white cloak of invisibility."

Then Seaspear took his leave of the king and queen and left with Sternrider and Winterwarrior to talk of warrior ships.

*****

CHAPTER FOUR
To the Islands of the Everyoung

When Snakeknife and Warchariot were alone and out of hearing they lowered their voices and made plans for war.

Snakeknife turned and sneered to Warchariot, "The four witches of kill have served us well for they have eaten the squirming, slippery eels of sly and cunning and soon the four fieldmarshals of the Wavewarriors will be enchanted away to the Islands of the Everyoung.

At this time, the four witches of kill brewed up strange visions in their fiery lair – visions that they controlled with odors and perfumes. These weird illusions from the other world were given form and substance by their potions. These ghosts were made alive to act in the world of man and so lead men astray into the mists of ocean. Such would be the fate of the fieldmarshals of the Wavewarriors, together with their foremost battle champions.

These brave heroes would leave the East, its islands and real seas, to stray into the flowers, plants and jungles of the illusionary Isles of the Everyoung. Thus all the islands of the Wavewarriors would lie at the mercy of Warchariot, King of the Eagle Warriors and his evil WarQueen Snakeknife. For what could one warrior do, even the young WarQueen Britania, against an army of Eagle Warriors?

Windweasel muttered to the other witches, "Little by little the way the tiny cat ate the big fish let us begin to scatter these Wavewarriors and their champions."

One day the Stormleaper saddled his hunting horse, a white horse like the great stallion Oceanhorse and rode out in the field to look for deer. Instead, he saw a young girl dressed in the armor and highboots of a warriorqueen riding a royal steed from out of the West. She wore a golden crown and a silk cloak of purple decked with dazzling silvery stars. She had skin whiter than the swan on water and her lips were softer than red wine mixed with honey. Her eyes were like the clear blue skies of summer. Two gold hoops hung from both her ears. Her hair was the same color as the hoops and flowed in thick locks over her shoulder. Her pink cheeks were like two peaches in bloom.

The warriorqueen pulled up her horse - a bay almost as big as the Great Bay of the West. Her steed was shod with silver and was harnessed in red bronze and in brown leather with golden smallbells tinkling as she rode along. His mane was gray and flowing in the wind as he shook his head and bowed in pride and friendship.

Stormleaper asked the girl, "Where do you come from?"

She answered him, "My father is the king of the Isle of the Everyoung. I had a vision that showed you to me. Your name is Stormleaper. Come with me to the Isles of the Everyoung and bring your warriors with you for company."

"But tell me who you are, besides a warriorqueen?" Stormleaper asked. "I see that you are beautiful but so are many – that is not enough for me to go with you."

The queen replied, "Then come and join me in the Isles of the Everyoung. You are free to leave at any time. And you will be protected by all your heroes. No one will entrap you. Take a small sip of red wine and if you find it good to drink, quaff the whole bottle. For you will find that I have many gifts. Besides the gift of beauty, I have the gift of voice and singing, of purity, of wisdom and witty conversation. My name is Tear for sadness and for joy. Your day will not be dull. It will be sunny."

Then Stormleaper laughed and told the queen, "I would not go with you unless you were able to keep above the talk of heroes but what is this far island of the sea where everything is young and lives forever? Would I be happy there? I am mature, a battle-hardened warrior of many wars."

"I say drink some wine and judge for yourself," she replied.

Tear plucked a blue flower from her cloak of silk and threw it at Stormleaper. He caught it and breathed its fragrance. Soon a vision rose around him of blues and reds and coral plants and rocks and streaming trees and birds of many colors.

The voice of Tear was so melodious and her beauty was so stunning that Stormleaper heard her words like one under a spell of silence. When she spoke, no bee buzzed in the flowers, no bird sang, no stream or river gurgled, no breeze rustled among the trees. A silence fell on all until she stopped speaking and the spell ended.

Stormleaper followed behind Tear with all his warriors until they reached the long sands of the sea. They galloped over high dunes of straggling grass, over the wet shore where tides had licked, over the wave crests sweeping out to the ocean, over the green seaweeded hills of turmoil into the slip and slide of heaving water.

They traveled like wind over the salt-sea smiling mountains of foam – followed by great seabirds flying in squadrons that cried aloud like crias, to warn the heroes who were following Tear. Through the rainbows and bright sunbeams they rode on through beaches lit by pearls and silvery fish all gleaming in the bright moonlight.

Far in the sky a vision arose before them of a huge panoramic view of war. The witch Windweasel appeared giving out cries of toothless, cruel laughter as her claws and skinny arms held closely to the reins and bridle of the Great Bay horse just like the stallion ridden by Queen Tear.

Then, opposite the Bay, a Seagull Warrior, wearing a purple cloak, pointed a spear at the old witch. Then an oriental warrior, mounted on the Great White Stallion Oceanhorse appeared. She was fully armored for combat. Above the two great horses flew the Mooncrow, circling above them.

It was not clear to Stormleaper and his men what this strange vision meant but it soon faded.

And Tear told them, "This is a sky picture of war. War is the last thing that you want or need." And Tear assured them that the tapestry in the air meant nothing but that a great war was coming soon.

Then the sky darkened into the grayish mists of cloud as all around grew dim and shivery as lightning stabbed them through and through. At last they left the blustery gale behind them and rode more gently into the warm Isles of the Everyoung – a land of sun and healing.

Queen Tear dismounted and welcomed Stormleaper and his champions, "Be happy for here there is no sorrow. Whatever you desire, it shall be yours."

The people of the Isles of the Everyoung were laughing and relaxed and welcoming. The land was full of rich blossoming trees of heavy blooms and humming, homing bees. Red, blue and green and yellow birds sang out and jumped and pecked in the green clover fields. The Everyoung were just as cheerful as those many-colored birds that ran and flew among the sunny branches of the forests. There, where the giant weeping willows wore green cloaks of shadeful leaves as shields from the hot sun.

So Stormleaper took Tear to be his queen and all his champions also took companions. Although Stormleaper did not long for the old ways for he was happy there with lovely Tear yet sometimes in the night he would rise out of his dreams and walk the warm paths of beauty in the night.

And so Stormleaper and his champions remained in a haze of warm sunlight in the Isles of the Everyoung.

***

One day Whaleroarer and his men were sailing around an island when a large ship was seen on the horizon. It was a long high craft of shining white with a carved crow upon the prow. The crow was the symbol of Whaleroarer's war battalion.

When his boat sailed close to the white ship they could not see anyone inside the ship except a beautiful red woman with red eyes and bright red hair. Her crimson hair hung loosely over her shoulders and blew back in the breeze. Her eyebrows were as black as crow and her eyes were like large rubies set in a blue-gray sky. Her long fingers were like red knives but tipped with sharp black dirks. She stood proudly aloft in the ship's prow as splashes of foam and wind blew fiercely around her.

The great sail on her ship that drove it forward was also emblazoned with a large black crow – the symbol of the hills and waterfalls division of the Seagull army - the crow flies up to perch on the pinnacles of springs and rapids.

Calm dignity and strength were in her voice as she raised one hand and pointed at Whaleroarer, "I am Sigh and I come from the Isles of the Everyoung, the Isle of Waterfalls and Rainbows. Come with me and bring all your heroes.

"Come to the dreamscape isles, the isle of hills and waterfalls and fountains where rainbows play and dance among the rapids, where the proud crow flies to the pinnacle of the high rocks."

Whaleroarer and his warriors were stunned as she sailed close then disappeared from view as her longboat shimmered and became a mist.

But when the mist cleared, blown by the sea breezes, they saw an ancient hag of withered skin – Rivershark, with her long white hair, was laughing as the Mooncrow, cawing and calling, flew up into the air and perched upon a tree branch.

Then Rivershark sneered and hid in the high tree watching the scene unfold of two great horses rearing up on their hind legs and snorting and beating with their hooves upon each other.

The vision was unclear and undulating but one horse was a White like Oceanhorse, the other was a Bay like Foresthorse. Now, in the vision, both were fighting fiercely and the Great White Stallion seemed to prevail. The Bay lay dead and many crows came down and flocked upon its body. They feasted upon its red flesh while the witch, Rivershark, sat in the tree and laughed with Mooncrow.

Slowly the vision faded from their sight like an intruder spying and then hiding.

Then Whaleroarer gave orders to pull away from shore and navigate out to far distant lands. Suddenly a cold storm blew and blocked their way. Great waves leapt up and screamed and waved their hands telling them, "Get back, get back." Each wave was like an army and a barrier. They heard the sound of a thousand tramping feet blocking their way as the great waves heaved, threatening to smash their boat into pieces, drowning Whaleroarer and his men.

Fear fell on all and even the brave Whaleroarer cried aloud, "If only we were on dry land, I swear I could defend myself against any warrior but against an army of the sea, I cannot."

As they heaved up and down they saw far out the beautiful Sigh in her longboat, sails full, approaching over the sea waves.

She came close to them and shouted, "What would you give if I should save you all?"

The warriors replied, "What do we have that you would want?"

She cried aloud to them, "Yourselves as my warriors."

And so Whaleroarer and his men gladly agreed as they followed her ship and were lured away to the other world.

Sigh sailed past them towards the Isle of Hills and all the seas beside her calmed and rested so that the heroes were able to follow her and row to a rivermouth that opened from the Isle of Waterfalls.

Taking the hand of Whaleroarer, she led them along the stream bank where green hills swept down to the clear crystal waters flowing over the sandy riverbed of small white pebbles. The stream was silvery bright and in it swam red speckled salmon. All around were pleasant wild woods of singing birds.

As they walked in the woods, red serving girls came out bearing bright drinking horns of wines while others sat far off and played on reeds in a low background breeze of forest music. They came to a wild orchard in the woods where the boughs were bending down with bright red apples. Scattered all around there were oak trees with green leaves and many acorn and hazel trees yellow with hazelnuts.

Sigh walked beside Whaleroarer as they climbed the hills that led to a great moor of flowers and bees and butterflies and honey where she showed him a white palace that shone in the blue sunlight.

And so Whaleroarer and his men were lured away to the illusiory Isles of the Everyoung.

**

Four buzzards flew down to the great snowy plain of the East and began to pick the dead that lay there after a skirmish between the Icedragon and horsethieves that came from the West.

Some horses had been stolen and some men had died upon the dusty buzzard plain. Seeing the buzzards picking the dead bodies, some of Icedragon's warriors muttered that this might be an omen of war, "Buzzards are often a symbol of death coming, sent by the powers of insight in the universe and the buzzard is the emblem of our division."

Icedragon nodded, "In that case, this is an omen of a coming victory for all the four divisions of our army not just our battalion. So be it."

The four buzzards disappeared from view giving way to the four witches of kill. Then the ground seemed to fall away beside them opening up a vast underground plateau filled with rainbows and warm jungles of bushes. A wide road opened up through this dream landscape.

Icedragon led the way through in his chariot to a place filled with pleasant streams and crystal fountains. In the far distance he could see the sea with the sun shining all around a sunny island that had appeared from nowhere out of a wide dusty plain of buzzards.

Icedragon glanced aside and saw two chariots, one on each side, riding along beside him. Each chariot was drawn by two bay horses just like the Great Red Bay of the Sternrider. The chariots were of wicker and steel with studs of silver and gold. Each of these two escorting chariots were driven by two warriorqueens – one warriorwoman for each of the two bays.

These warriorqueens wore armor, helmets and shields, along with all the accoutrements of combat. One of the warriorqueens had eyes like meteors, just like the eyes of the witch Meteoreyes, just like two burning furnaces of fire. All four of these well-armed and deadly warriorwomen were lithe and muscular. Each was tall, sharp, elegant and young-faced with thick and curly yellow hair flowing from underneath bronze helmets. All had nails like sharp black daggers at their fingertips and their teeth were white as pebbles when they spoke.

One of the warriorqueens spoke to Icedragon. Her eyes were grey-blue, calm and clear and thoughtful, not enflamed like meteors.

"My name is Smile and smiling is for joy or for wry wit and I can bring you both, if you should choose to come with me. You are an icecold warrior with neither joy nor wit and it is known that most men worship all those fine qualities they do not have themselves. However, this is for you to choose."

Icedragon replied coldly, "Tell us now, what are the ways of life in this strange place?"

Then Queen Smile turned her chariot to the West and her companion chariot went with her. Icedragon and his champions followed her through thick orchards and purple jungles. They galloped across the plain through rainbows and tall flowers until they arrived at the land where Queen Smile ruled. The palace was filled with strangely scented flowers that stung the nostrils and caused a mist to appear in a large hall where two thrones stood.

While the Icedragon breathed in this strong smell, the mist changed into the form of the witch Landslink who writhed and transformed into a huge buzzard. As the mist wafted away she took the appearance of

Queen Smile, a beautiful woman with golden skin and hair.

"Come sit upon this golden throne Icedragon and I will show you visions. You can become the greatest fieldmarshal."

And so Icedragon and his champions were all lured away to the illusory Isles of the Everyoung.

***

One dark night an old witch visited the castle of Summersailor. She was dressed in a black cowl wrapped closely around her head. She drove a burnt black chariot that looked as though it had been driven through the pit and set on fire by demons. It was pulled by two black horses with red eyes of fire and likewise the witch had eyes of fiery flame. She told the gatemen that she sold good luck.

A gateman asked her, "How high is your price?"

She replied, "I ask only a prayer. I give only a blessing."

He was stunned and let her through into the inner courtyard for she had let him smell her stinging flowers of illusion so that he feared her vengeance and bad luck. The witch was Meteoreyes and her stock in trade was the medicine of delusion and false dreams. She had a cage of evil songbirds with her that sang a song of dreaming and mindmadness.

At the same time Summersailor was asleep with his champions resting nearby when he was visited by a beautiful young Woman of the Sea who suddenly appeared before him smiling. "Do not be fearful. My name is Laugh. I am a child of joy and laughter and a warriorwoman from the Isle of Farsky one of the Islands of the Everyoung.

"Do you remember how you got your name – brave Summersailor? When you were a child of only five you pleaded for the chance to sail alone and unaccompanied for you were living with your foster family, to train you as a warrior. They asked your father for permission for you to sail alone and unaccompanied only in summer until you reached the age of ten. Then you would also be allowed to sail in winter.

"Then I watched you sail alone on the high seas and so admired your courage that I swore that when you grew up I would visit you and offer you my heart – and this I do. Now some strange power has released me to make this longed-for visit to entreat you."

Summersailor thought back to his early childhood. "I do remember that hawks flew overhead when I was a boy just learning to sail. Where do you come from?"

"I am a hawk, a seawoman. We live on the Islands of the Everyoung. The sea is my blue garden grown with fruit. When you think that you are sailing on the sea, among the small green waves of summertime, I see a planted wood of birds and leaves when I drive out brightly in the sun upon my chariot pulled by sea-horses. You see the prow of your longboat through the snow-white waves throwing the spray about. I see only, as I ride the waves, fine fields with daisies growing all around. You see the wood of your longboat that smells like salt seaweed and makes you deeply sigh. I see a wood of hazelnuts and chestnuts surrounded by red flowers that smell of wine. I see the woods that will not pass away nor die to winter's blight of snow and cold.

"Come with me now Summersailor," she begged him.

So Summersailor got into her chariot where a strange transformation seized him and he felt younger and his sight more sharp and all around were happy, cheerful faces of the hawk people and his own friends and champions. Proudly the horses pranced. The chariots rocked backward and forward over the green waves of grass and soil and flowers of the sea just as the Queen of Laugh had promised. The seahorses shook their manes and bowed and flicked their tails from side to side as Laugh lured away Summersailor and his champions to the Land of the Young.

***

After the old witch had lured away Summersailor and all his champions, she lit a small fire just below the tower and burnt her flowers under the high windows. In the room above, Whitehair, the young niece of Summersailor lay fast asleep. Her father was dead and her mother was Purplelake the sister of King Waterbear. The smoke and the smell of the devil flowers that drifted upwards in the twilight carried hallucination and deceit.

When the girl woke up and looked out of her high window she saw the sameshape of her uncle. Whitehair had the gift of discerning spirits but was overcome by the visions and the sounds and the smell of the delusional smoke and flowers. Soon she was seized away in a sleepful haze as the gray witch led the child out into the black chariot pulled by a pair of coal black stallions. This took them to the castle of the four witches of kill in the distant woods where they lived and schemed.

So Whitehair was bound with chains and locked away in the cellar of the castle to remain there until she was needed to be a hostage or until she grew up to be used to receive a transplant of the brain of Meteoreyes bringing new life and a new body to that witch of kill.

*****

CHAPTER FIVE
Britania Stands Alone

As the witches consulted together in their castle, Landslink spoke up, "Now is the right time for the Eagle Warriors to launch a war against the Wavewarriors. Their four fieldmarshals and all their champions have been lured away to the Isles of Youth. Let us send messengers to Warchariot and his WarQueen Snakeknife telling them it is safe to launch attacks to steal all the horses from the East leaving their chariots to rot and rust. The Eagles need only to hold fast to Seaspear for the Seagull Warriors to become totally isolated without their heroes and champions."

So Seaspear chose to go on ruling all the ships under King Warchariot's command but he remained restless and disturbed in sleep and in his walks from dream to dream.

Without her champions and heroes, the young Britania stood alone in her chariot with only her servants beside the straits that link up East and West. There at the sign of cria and the sea, at low tide, it became a sandy isthmus.

The four fieldmarshals and their chief heroes of the Seagulls had gone to seek long life in the dream jungles of the far western Isles of the Everyoung.

Gentleleaf had gone to join Seaspear in his sailing ship where he was now a fieldmarshal in the Eagle camp.

Her younger brother Stormbolt lived with the Kim family in the East and was being trained by Shadowhero in the skills of combat.

Purplelake, sister of Summersailor, had gone alone to find Whitehair who was last seen with the witch Meteoreyes.

So Warchariot gathered together all the Eagle army into the thick bushes west of the swift straits. Britania stalked at night among the Eagles, killing and mutilating and beheading among the war camps of the gathering foes. As she sowed the seeds of terror in the darkness, the Eagles became fearrattled and bone-jittery.

Meanwhile, Seaspear heard a rumor that the horses of the East were going to be stolen so he sent a warning to her. So Britania secretly sent some of her servants to drive away and hide as many horses as they could so that the horsethieves of Warchariot would flee away empty handed.

To get back to their army, the five horsethieves had to pass over the swift straits between East and West. They knew that she was nearby, so they hid in the forest until she was asleep. When Britania sent some of her Seagulls to find them and point them out, crias flew overhead and swooped down on the heads of the horsethieves causing them to scream out loud showing their exact location. She threw javelins and transfixed four of them to the trees and cut their heads off with her battle axe.

The fifth horsethief surrendered to Britania, who told him, "Line the heads up on your chariot and stick them upon the spikes along the back. In this way, they will grin and grimace to the crowds of Eagles as you drive through your camp. Drive them right through the soldiers of your army until you reach the campsite where your Queen Snakeknife sits with King Warchariot. There they sit, unaware of danger, under the roof of shields held by their bodyguards. Until you do so I will stand upon that rock and watch you. If you do not deliver, you will receive this javelin through your chest. I want the Eagles and their king and queen to see what I have set aside for them."

The fifth horsethief assured her, "I swear I will do as you say."

The horsethief drove his chariot with the severed heads over the straits into the bushland of the Eagle armies but when he reached his friendly front battalion, he felt at home and safe among his fellows and, not wanting to display the severed heads as a boasting for Britania, he left his chariot with the heads aloft and ran to meet his fieldmarshal Sternrider.

However, he fell down prostrated on his face, his hands almost touching the leader's feet, his face screwed up with blood, his mouth gasping and his chest pinned down by the sharp javelin of Britania who did what she had promised.

Then Sternrider bore the news to WarQueen Snakeknife who quietly muttered to Warchariot, "We cannot win this war while Britania is there – she bars our way, whether the island lies as low-tide or high-tide. For when the tide is high it rushes freely, sweeping along the warboats and the skiffs and when the tide is low it drains away and leaves a path of sand where only one warrior at a time may pass, such is the slippery nature of that path. Coming or going is for her to say. If we would steal their warhorses as planned, we must remove her from the straits. But who will now be forced to face this madness? Who wants to stand against a warriorwoman who fights alone and singlehanded against the mightiest army in the world? Who would stand up in single combat against a solitary hero like the young WarQueen Britania?"

Sternrider answered, "I will find a man of courage or a warrior who is seeking to make his name, a gloryseeker who needs to be a winner, a cool blade who would fight a rabid lion."

"You are very wise Sternrider," said Snakeknife.

But when Sternrider went out to seek his best champions, Snakeknife muttered to the king, "Sternrider is too direct and honest. We don't need a champion to fight Britania. Let us call upon the help of the Queen of Justice who can send sly and cunning killers against her.

So while Britania stood alone in her chariot in the middle of the slow green seaweeded sea with sand and bushes and a gray shrubbery lying all around on both sides of the isthmus, the deadly creatures came upon Britania ready to sneak upon her with spears.

Unluckily for these quiet assassins, crawling their way along the grassy sandunes, the crias were crying aloud in fear above them for they were treading among the crias hidden eggs and sand nests. As the screaming crias swooped down and hit the heads of each disguised assassin, Britania shot each assassin dead with an arrow.

While she was dealing with these attacks, other Eagle warriors rode by and stole some horses. So she cried out to the Sternrider, "Send out to me one warrior who has the courage to fight me face-to-face, one at a time in one-to-one combat. I will allow your forces to advance, even to steal some horses from us but only as long as the one-to-one combat lasts."

Sternrider approached the straits in his chariot. Politely he nodded with respect to her, "Britania, my greetings go to you. Please know that these killers were not sent by me – that is not my form. Those slinking assassins were sent to you by the strange seer known as Justice Queen who predicted a victory for them."

Britania laughed aloud.

Sternrider smiled, "I fear that war is building up between us in spite of all our honorable efforts. Your four fieldmarshals leaving you appears to many to have destroyed your army. You are defenseless but I will find a warrior worthy of you, as you have asked. One who will not need cunning, one who will combat with you one-to-one.

Three fierce and powerful warriors stood before WarQueen Snakeknife and King Warchariot, they were the three Drumnecks, brothers and veterans of combat. They looked exactly like each other with their battlegear, armor, helmets and their black cloaks. Three gorillas, hairy and ugly, bony and odorous, were never more alike.

Sternrider, bowed low before the king and queen, "Here I present three brothers for the battle against the hopeless and alone, Britania. They have agreed to fight her one at a time, no ganging up on her, all single combat.

"In return, she has agreed that, while they struggle on, our armies will be free to press ahead perhaps for three days. Otherwise, no one would come to stand against her and she would never have a chance to defeat us and defend the East from our fierce Eagle Warriors. It is better for us to lose one man at a time rather than to be destroyed with heavy losses, for her swift sword would soon mow down large numbers of our men."

Then Queen Snakeknife addressed the Drumnecks.

"I feel sure that you will kill Britania but do not underrate her powers of kill. It would give heart to others to go against her if you could even touch the eastern shore after your battle. Even if a warrior won such a token victory and died, his memory and his family would be honored."

Displeased with these words, the eldest Drumneck spoke with arrogance, "I have no intention of leaving my body anywhere. I intend to leave the bones of Britania out there and to come home alone to receive honors, as I have always done."

Sternrider and the king and queen were eager to calm the pride of the Drumnecks, so they nodded in sure approval, "But of course you shall have honor, popular acclaim, a writing of approval and gallantry, fine words of praise on a small plaque of bronze signed in engravement by the king and queen."

The Drumnecks set their faces hard against Britania and looked pleased as they strode away like three cocks strutting in the early morning to cock-a-doodle-do at the first dawn.

After they had gone, the Great Bay horse ridden by Sternrider crossed over the straits and hid, ready and waiting. He drove a great herd of horses led by the Great White Stallion over the straits from East to West. These stolen horses were then hidden away to be used later in the coming war campaign with chariots, against the Wavewarriors.

A great crowd of the curious Eagles gathered to watch the contest between the Drumnecks and Britania.

The Drumnecks, breaking their word that they would fight one at a time in single combat, now threw themselves in fury at Britania. Two strode in front, holding their shields to hide the third who sneaked upon her with a great axe. The two with shields holding a grip of spears and javelins then ran one to each side one north the other south. Britania turned her chariot with speed just as the spears and javelins were flying so that they tore into the chariot's backboard. At the same time she jumped out into the shallow waters of the strait and leapt upon the Drumneck who wielded the axe, cutting his head off with a sword. Then she seized a spear out of the backboard of her chariot and flung it through the heart of number two as the third Drumneck rushed forward with his sword but Britania threw her broad sword with such force that it went through the shield and body armor into the heart of the third Drumneck.

As he splashed around bleeding and dying, he screamed out to the terrified observers, "I claim the eastern shore though I am dying. All of you can come later to fulfill my claim. See this left hand of victory and in my good right hand a sword of war."

The Drumneck splashed and crawled upon the shore of the Eastland and died, clutching the soil. Britania walked over in her fury and severed the hands and feet of the Drumneck who made the arrogant claim to victory. Then she cut off both the hands and feet of the other Drumnecks who had broken faith and threw them all into her chariot.

She drove to the shore of the Eagle camp and smeared her chariot all around with gumtree syrup and covered it with dead seaweed and branches and dried leaves all around the top and sides and back of its wood canopy.

Then she set fire to the whole chariot and drove it fiercely through the camp of Eagles and threw the hands and feet of the Drumnecks onto the ground beside the main campfire, crying out, "Those who wish to follow the war claim of the Drumnecks, let him know that the same fate awaits him as these hands that cannot hold and the same fate awaits him as these feet that cannot walk."

As she drove back her fiery chariot, WarQueen Snakeknife and King Warchariot declared, "The three Drumnecks have honor, popular acclaim – a writing of approval and gallantry to be inscribed upon a plaque of bronze." But the Eagles who heard these words were silent and evasive as they stood beside the sea, watching the crias.

Then Warchariot and Snakeknife called a conference with Seaspear and Sternrider to find a way to deal with Britania.

Sternrider said, "So far I have tried hard to keep our conflict honorable. I am sorry that the three champions we sent against Britania were frauds and losers. Seaspear, you have a foot in both our camps.

Why don't you choose a warrior who would be fierce enough to fight against Britania?"

But Seaspear shook his head, "I am impartial because Britania is my niece. My task is only to keep this war from getting any worse. We must try to reverse this enmity before the Eagle Warriors and the Wavewarriors destroy each other. Let us have a truce – a time for talk. "

"Yes, I do agree," said the cunning Snakeknife, "but men cannot or will not do the talking, so I will meet with one of their main warriorwomen and try to calm things."

All four agreed.

Seaspear was pleased and added, "The sister of Summersailor, Purplelake, will be back in a few days from her search to find Whitehair."

"Has Whitehair wandered off?" asked Snakeknife, who knew that the four witches had kidnapped Whitehair and were holding her as a hostage.

Seaspear replied, "That young woman has the gift of being able to discern dark spirits – only strong magic could have stolen her."

Snakeknife frowned and shook her head and thought, "When she returns from searching for her child perhaps I could truce-talk with Purplelake. Until then, we must find a warrior to hold the battle against Britania. So Seaspear, send us some of your best men of the Eagles and we will choose between them so that there will be no conflict for you. We understand that no Wavewarrior will go against her."

Seaspear did so but remained worried and uneasy. "No warrior could stand against Britania," he told the king and queen.

They all nodded politely.

Sternrider, too, was thoughtful and disturbed.

So the Eagle Warrior chosen to fight Britania was Gripstone who was promised his own fighting ship.

"I need a ship to attack Britania for she has a chariot and the Great White Stallion."

"Agreed," said Warchariot, "You shall have a ship from which to attack Britania. If the ship is damaged in the fierce combat, then you shall have another when you return. Then I will raise you to the rank of

Vi-King to show the world you are an honored champion."

The Eagle Warrior was well pleased and bowed humbly before the king and queen, then went to supervise his ship. It was to be rowed by Eagle Warriors. Inside the ship among the weapons were loud singing shields that screamed a warning when the foe came near.

The Queen of Justice went to speak to Gripstone to encourage him to take part in the combat. She made a false prophecy, "It is foredoomed that Britania will fall. Here is a parrot that repeats my words from far away so if my foresight changes it will inform you. You will be forewarned."

Gripstone was happy to receive the parrot and tied it to his shoulder strap. It cawed and croaked, "WarQueen Britania will die before Gripstone."

When Gripstone sailed his longboat into the straits at the high tide, Sternrider sent his thieves across the sea to round up herds of horses hidden among the bushes and the forests.

While brave Britania waited alone for Gripstone at the straits, she saw several crows fly up in the distance. She knew that they had been disturbed and frightened by the hooves of sudden moving herds of horses. Because she had to make a firm stand against Gripstone there was nothing more that she could do to stop the horsethieves driving off the stallions.

But she was helped by the fierce seas that rose up. It was as though those seas knew that Britania was in need as they came to the defense of the young WarQueen of the Wavewarriors. The waves turmoiled into a mighty wall of combat to drive back all the stallions and the horsethieves.

It is strange how nature sometimes echoes the person for nature is often in full harmony with man.

Then she stepped back from the great waves and threw two javelins. One of the javelins went through the parrot that perched on the shoulder of Gripstone while it shouted, "WarQueen Britania will die before Gripstone."

The other javelin pierced the steering wheel and sank deep into the hard wooden deck of Gripstone's ship, locking the wheel in place so that the ship could not be steered in time to master the high waves. The ship was doomed to crash against the nearby rocks. It perished and all the weapons fell to the sea bottom and sank into the sand.

The seamen swam back to the western shore and told the king, "The weather was against us; the seas rose despite the good predictions of the parrot given us by the Justice Queen."

Warchariot sneered, "Only a fish would trust a parrot." Then he ordered all the wrecked seamen to be beheaded.

Now Gripstone also swam to the western shore after his ship was wrecked upon the rocks. But he stood firm against Britania and called to her across the straits, "Come choose your weapons, for you are the only one who has been challenged."

Britania sat high upon her chariot drawn by two seahorses, prancing and plunging; their manes and tails swishing and flowing like the salt sea foam that flies and sprays the air.

"You have lost most of your weapons in the sea but I will give you what you need," said Britania.

"I want nothing from you except your life," replied Gripstone. "Now choose your deadly weapon."

"If I could have my choice, I would choose my hands and wring your neck – it is so stiff and arrogant," said Britania.

Gripstone replied, "No weapons are the best weapons of all; no armor is the best protection, too, for that will make us all the more determined to see the best warrior win at hand-to-hand."

The Mooncrow screeched and cawed in hatred as both left their weapons and armor on the shore and plunged into the sea. A slithery seasnake was set loose by the Mooncrow upon Britania. It wound itself around her legs and tripped her so that she fell backwards just as Gripstone was flinging himself forward at brave Britania. As Gripstone fell forward and lost his balance, Britania was able to seize him by the throat and throttle him with both hands under the water.

Then she stood up and tore the seasnake off, holding it up and crushing it in her hand. She threw it at the Eagle camp and shouted, "Here is a dead snake, take it to your live one."

But no Eagle did, for fear of their evil WarQueen Snakeknife.

Then Britania armed herself for battle against the horsethieves and drove her chariot towards the circling crows. For now that the waters were abating somewhat, the thieves were still trying to round up horses and drive them over the straits to join the Eagles. The horses chomped and neighed and near stampeded among the trees and bushes to escape the cruel whips and goads of the horsethieves.

The crows and other birds were still disturbed and flocking high and circling over the trees. Britania could see them up above the trees and bushes and soon she fell upon the horsethieves and slew them swiftly, letting one escape to tell the story to their king – Warchariot.

Then she swiftly drove her chariot to her ship and sailed away to rejoin her fellow Seagull Warriors.

*****

CHAPTER SIX

Revenge

When these things were reported to Warchariot, his evil WarQueen Snakeknife was furious and called a meeting with her Justice Queen.

"We have the greatest army and one warrior takes our strategy apart. We need to get their horses on our side before their champions return. This Britania can read the signs of nature and act like a small army on her own.

"So Britania has sailed away - I knew it. We need to match her with a deadly warrior and none of your omens have helped us, Justice Queen. You need to use your brains, think of a plan."

"Of course and I will do so, Queen Snakeknife. It would be bad if we should lose our hostage young Whitehair and I hear that her mother, Purplelake, is determined to find her. If I could say that you had found clues to the whereabouts of Whitehair, a secret meeting could be arranged between the great Queen Snakeknife of the Eagles and Purplelake somewhere unknown to Britania. Also do you really need more horses?"

"Of course not," replied Snakeknife, "but we need to keep them out of the way of the Wavewarriors."

So the Justice Queen suggested to Snakeknife that they kill the horses. "Why should we kidnap these animals? This puts us to great trouble and expense for nothing. Britania cannot drive away dead horses."

At that moment Snakeknife shook her head and exclaimed, "You have exposed me as a mere softie. I am not ruthless enough; I swear that I will try to be more cruel in the future. Of course the horses must be killed and set up that meeting between me and Purplelake."

Unknown to Britania, Purplelake walked into the snare laid out by the false Justice Queen - the fly was Purplelake the spider was Snakeknife.

So it was that the Queen of Justice came to visit Purplelake late after dark and talked to her in secret, "I think that Queen Snakeknife knows about the disappearance of your daughter Whitehair who is being held hostage. If the war goes badly for the Eagles, Whitehair may be exchanged for a queenly sum of money. Warriors can solve things only with the force of arms but we women are more subtle and devious. Queen Snakeknife is mainly interested in wealth. Perhaps you could pay more for Whitehair than the price demanded by Warchariot and so get back your daughter now. But I will also need a small fee for my services."

So Purplelake paid the Justice Queen her small fee and went with her by night and in secret, though curious servants listened at the door. The sly Queen Snakeknife hid her assassins and then went to speak with Purplelake in a bright moonlit clearing in the woods. "Are you still searching for your daughter Whitehair?"

"I will keep looking for her till the day I die," replied Purplelake.

"That is so sad," said Snakeknife, "I feared as much for now I must bring your misery to an end." And with that the evil WarQueen Snakeknife signaled to the javelineers who stood by in the shadows.

***

Britania slept uneasily and awoke like a prisoner breaking out of a black dungeon then decked herself in the accoutrements of war. Like a cock striding out in the cold dawn she saw, far from the straits, grey forms of buzzards descending out of dull clouds – the scavengers of death, circling around and waiting for a chance to swoop upon their prey and eat the bodies. Six buzzards were prepared to come down upon a scene of slaughter and desecration.

When she untied the Great White Stallion, it broke away and galloped to the scene of death from which the smoke curled slowly upwards. Britania followed the Great White Stallion, harnessing black and grey horses in her battle chariot. When she arrived at the scene of the buzzards, the

Great White was stampeding at the head of a large herd of horses that had panicked to escape the spears and javelins of the horsethieves.

The horsethieves had been told to kill the horses and many broken bodies of fine animals were lying there – victims of the spears. As the escape stampede galloped away, led by the White, some of the thieves and murderers were crushed to death by the hooves of the wild stallions. Far away the Great Bay horse retreated, abandoning his sortie on the horses of the East as he had tried to block their path.

The horsethieves had been hacking at an oak to block the road of access to the scene of death. Even as the oak tree fell across the path, Britania rode her horses high and cleared the oak tree, chariot and all, crashing and clattering on the other side.

As the horse assassins fled, she beheaded each of them as they screamed and begged for mercy. One of them cried aloud, "We only did what the Justice Queen commanded."

A light snow stream fell upon the bodies of men and horses, like the pall that covers a palace when a king draws near to it on a winter's night.

Then Britania followed the horses that had been led to safety by the White. She paused and looked back at the men and horses that lay there dead under the pall of snow with buzzards coming for their prey.

Meanwhile, Seaspear still wanted a just end to the war – a peace talk to bring honor to both sides but his wife, Queen Gentleleaf, reminded him that Whitehair had been taken by the witches of kill.

"They say she is dead but I do not believe their lies. Purplelake has also disappeared and there are rumours that she went with the Justice Queen to search for Whitehair."

Seaspear replied, "I will go and speak to Snakeknife and Warchariot and make it clear whose army I support."

So he went to talk to Queen Snakeknife and said, "Britania is a strong warrior who cannot be defeated. Let us back off this war for no good can come of it. You cannot win."

But Snakeknife cried, "No way. She is one body and can be overcome, omens have told us. Also, their four fieldmarshals with all their crack battalions are far away in the Islands of the Everyoung. The victory could be ours if only we could find one man to kill one woman – is that too much to ask?"

Seaspear replied, "It is not up to me to choose a man. I am only an admiral to help seamen with skills of seamanship. Ask your advisor the Queen of Justice if she wishes to meet with Britania, to trucetalk with her. It may be that peace will triumph unless you wish to talk of peace yourself."

But Snakeknife feared that word of all her murders would soon leak out and she chose not to go.

***

So Seaspear sent word to the Queen of Justice to come and talk with Britania but she was troubled and went to the Mooncrow for a read of omens.

Mooncrow flew down, took the form of a hag and led a strange monkey with her and three vials of foresight.

"Drink these vials of prophecy, then take this monkey of prognosis with you and keep it on your back."

The Justice Queen drank and let the monkey climb upon her shoulder. At once she saw a vision of dead horses – the view that Britania had seen earlier.

Then she went to Seaspear and told him, "The omen is not good. Dead horses of the East lay all around and I fear that Britania will kill all against her, even the women."

"Prophecies are not always true," said Seaspear, "and I swear that if Britania or any man even tries to wound you, I will take their head."

"Will you ride beside me in your chariot to keep the peace?"

Seaspear swore, "I will and I will send them word that I am coming."

When Britania received word from Seaspear of his coming, she dressed in body armor and full weapons of self-defense like a true warriorwoman including a hard shield which no sharp javelins could pierce.

When Seaspear arrived with the Queen of Justice he left his chariot and went to speak with some of the Seagull Warriors.

The Queen of Justice held a round shield before her and on her back the monkey of prognosis clung with its arms tightly around her throat. As they stood at the back of Seaspear's chariot, the monkey grinned and flashed its fine white teeth.

When the Queen of Justice suggested to Britania that they should talk about a peace, Britania carefully and deliberately selected her sharpest javelin and threw it swiftly at the Justice Queen and the monkey pinning them hard to the backboard of the chariot. As the sharp weapon fatally pierced her heart, the seer gave a loud gasp and clutched the javelin as though she needed its support to stand. The demons of the air, the fiends of war and the strange twisted cries of wayward weapons gone astray screamed out and then fell silent.

Before she died she spoke with her last breath, "Why did you do this, before I had a chance to speak of peace?"

"Because of Purplelake and all the dead horses," replied Britania. "Those brave and obedient warhorses were willing to risk their lives to help us in the battle but you had them all destroyed. Then speak of peace, for now you die of war."

The Queen of Justice fell forward in the chariot revealing the monkey still stuck upon the board with its mouth and eyes still staring.

When Seaspear came back from his talks he mounted his chariot without a word. He sighed and grimly shook his head as he drove back to the Eagle camp with the monkey and seer still shaking and transfixed on the backboard of his chariot.

***

Then Britania threw out her javelin at random into the nearby camp of Warchariot and pierced Warchariot's ancient mother, Spiderlair, bringing great fear among the Eagle Warriors.

"She will kill all of us, even the women, if we allow her," they cried.

Snakeknife searched desperately for a warrior who would challenge the young WarQueen of the Wavewarriors.

Then Britania called out, "Send me a man to stand alone before me. I want no more horsethieves or cowardly murderers. Send me five men at once or even ten."

Queen Snakeknife sent out ten warriors in full armor with swords and helmets. Each held a spear that they flung at Britania with deadly aim. She caught ten spears on her shield, mounted her chariot and swung her sword, the short thick sword that hacked its way through arms and legs and necks. She slashed and cut all ten like a great butcher cutting up ten pigs.

When King Warchariot was told what had happened he became disoriented and shook from head to toe. He unscrewed his index finger with the long sharp nail and told his warriors, "Be firm and do not yield to Britania. Her herolight is shining and she berserks and turmoils in her mind. I wish that we had not destroyed her horses nor even allowed you, Snakeknife, to destroy Purplelake. It has cost us more than we have gained by it."

Snakeknife was silent as Warchariot continued, "Let us lie awake and wait for her to come in darkness then we can seize her in the dead of night."

But Britania climbed into her battle chariot with its scythed wheels and launched a fierce attack that evening on the warcamp of the Eagles in revenge for the murder of the horses.

A great noise arose as the demons yelled and ghosts awoke and screamed who had not lived for many hundred years. The Mooncrow laughed like a flying hag. Like a crone of filth she flew overhead and cursed the battle scene. The strife that the devils stirred was loud, hard and ear-piercing. It stabbed the ears like the strike of a sharp arrow. The fiends of war flew over Britania and called on her to kill and slake their thirst for human blood. The Eagle camp shook with a trembling running through the blood.

A great anger came upon Britania as she saw the huge numbers of EagleWarriors and no champions or heroes to stand beside her. She stood up in her war chariot, grasping two javelins, her shield and sword and swung the sword and beat upon her shield until it rang with an ear-spitting din. She whirled her spear and cried aloud with anger that shook the blood and trembled the heart.

The Eagle enemy became insane with fear and confusion as they seized their weapons in the darkness and flung themselves in panic and disorder upon the swords and spearpoints of their friends. As chaos reigned they stabbed out at each other killing their comrades and families in the dead of night. The buzzards of the sea flew down and smelling the dead bodies of men and women they gorged themselves and gloated in the blood.

Britania woke up like a cock at the screech of dawn and strode into her armored chariot drawn by the Great White Stallion. She wore the cloak of speed and shadow vision that came upon her briefly when she was angry. So swift and furious was her chariot-run that it soon blurred into invisibility.

Then she called on a charioteer, "I have challenged that great army to send me one man who can stand before me and no one has stepped forward. So now I want you to take me on a tour of battle to treat this army as a field of corn and cut it down like harvest in the fall."

The charioteer wore his armor and mail over a stiff, hard deerskin tunic and sharp studded amulets with steel stud gloves. He took the whips and goads and crouched over the reins and reared the two great stallions into a gallop as they snorted great clouds of steam with sparks of fire. Then he drove them towards the Eagle battle camp.

Britania wore her ridged and studded steel Helmet of Cry that screamed insults and threats. The warriors of the Eagles were cut down by her sharp sword and shield. They fell in rows heaped high upon each other's bodies as the charioteer crouched low behind the horses on his yoketrap steering the smoking chariot like a death machine along the rows of dead piled high on either side.

The arms, heads and legs of hound and horse and human, grinning and twisted, challenged those who passed by, "Guess who I am, this is a masquerade and guess who this skull belonged to when it lived?" But the piles of bodies brought no answer back. And so Britania carved out a bloody path among the Eagles.

So great was the slaughter that the fieldmarshal of the Eagles, Sternrider, took up his chariot drawn by the Great Bay Stallion and drove out onto the field to stop the mayhem but he could not come anywhere near to Britania, so high were the piles of dead stacked up on every side.

Again Britania ploughed a wide circuit all around the Eagles just to make sure that none of them escaped without having to face her death-machine. Not all the Eagles died but all fought hard to stay alive and some lost limbs or eyes.

After this rout, King Warchariot and his vile Queen Snakeknife sent for Sternrider and told him, "Stop this slaughter or we will hold you personally responsible for the war."

Sternrider replied, "I will fight with Britania face-to-face but we must take time to rest our warriors from this great onslaught."

Though it seemed that Britania was tired, wounded and worn out after her great circuit against the Eagles, Sternrider showed no haste to lead his men against her. Meanwhile the hawks flew up and watched the buzzards pick the bones on the fields of carnage.

***

Britania drove to her island fastness where she fell into a troubled sleep, walking in that moving landscape where the present and the past and future meet.

When she awoke from her sleep she cried out in despair and one of her servants touched her forehead and spoke quietly, "Be calm you have been wounded and feel that all is lost and that you are alone. Our four fieldmarshals and their heroes have gone, there is the disappearance of Whitehair, the death of Purplelake and the theft of our horses. Is there a plot behind all this? I wish we could find the wisdom we need to sieze the key to victory."

Then her lady-in-waiting went to the high window and saw the far tents and war camps of the Eagles. As she looked and wept over the fields of a hundred thousand Eagles in the camps, she cried out, "I can see a lean, tall man. He walks with pride and his eyes look straight ahead. His shoulders are erect, he breathes with ease. But no one in all that camp is looking at him or even seems aware of his presence."

Suddenly the Truthteller stood in the room before them. There hung beside his belt a sheaf of golden darts of truth. These darts were deadly, never failing to kill when striking at the heart of any liar.

"Britania, I am the Truthteller, your godfather and now you must sleep for four days to heal your wounds and I will leave for your healing in sleep flowers, ferns and tree leaves for your recovery.

"I tell you, though you have done well and valiantly in making the great circuit to terrorize and cut down all your foes, yet you must learn that wars should not be won, only by dealing death. Pacts and alliances are also needed. You must make good deals and honest and honorable bargains when you can for not all foes are liars and deceivers. The Eagles are relieved to know that you are lying sick. They wish you dead.

"So that they will not think you weak or vanquished – for you are not, rather you will be victorious – I will walk through the Eagle camp again to my home far in the ocean. This time they will see me coming and when they do they will think they see the young WarQueen Britania with her golden hair, dressed in her weapons and accoutrements. I will not fight for you for it is wrong that I should take sides in a human war. But I can let them see the truth that you are still alive and waiting to return to raid the Eagles as you did before."

Then the Truthteller took the helmet, weapons and all the accoutrements of battle combat that she had worn and kissed the hand of Britania then walked away much as he had come, through the Eagle camp still performing tricks of sword and dirk and javelin, sharp backward jumps and the catching of spears and knives. When the Eagle Warriors saw him coming they fled. Some threw their spears and javelins from afar but these did not touch Truthteller so that the legend grew that the young WarQueen Britania was indestructible and could not be killed.

*****

CHAPTER SEVEN
Sternrider's Double Deal

King Warchariot and his WarQueen Snakeknife set up a council to get advice from their fieldmarshals.

The question is "How do we stop Britania?" asked Warchariot, "Or again, which one of you will kill the young WarQueen, Britania?"

Seaspear cried out, "I know what not to do. Do not kill their horses unless you want Britania to destroy us all."

Then Seaspear became silent and paused to think about this for some time.

Winterwarrior spoke up, "I will obey Sternrider's orders, knowing he will never ask me to do what he would not do first. But if I may make a humble contribution, I think we might try offering Britania supplies. She is honor bound to help protect her people from the cold and the snows and winds of winter hunger."

"Just so," replied Warchariot, "But first, to make that work we need to wreak more havoc upon the eastern lands."

Sternrider suggested, "I do agree with Winterwarrior here. We seek supremacy over eastern lands and all their peoples but I do not want to ride over a graveyard that never has been known to raise good crops. Perhaps if we could make a claim of triumph, even a gesture of formal victory, such as a finger or an ear of Britania, this would be enough to turn the tide of war and stir our troops to fighting with more hope."

"Just as easy to kill her as take an ear," sneered Snakeknife, "but we'll take what we can get."

"Very well, then we are all agreed," responded Sternrider, "I will lead a small crack company against Britania. I will fight her alone in single combat and when I rout

Britania, you should be ready to invade behind me. Is this agreed?"

All agreed with this. Their worried and fearful faces became brightsmiled as they bowed and shook the hand of Sternrider.

So Sternrider lead a small but deadly company down to the straits, picking a hidden place shaded by rocks from wind and waves and spies.

Britania approached the straits fully weaponed for combat to meet with the Sternrider on the field of battle.

Sternrider told his men, "Lay hidden while I negotiate with Britania and be ready to back me up if I call on you."

Then Sternrider approached Britania with respect, his sword undrawn and his daggers in their scabbards. He motioned to his servants to come forward with a drinking horn of red wine and a plate of silver salmon.

"I wish to talk to you," he told Britania.

She agreed, "Let us be brief. This is no time for wine drinking or feasting."

"Agreed," said Sternrider, "these tokens are only the symbols of respect and honor between us two."

"I do agree," said Britania.

"I have always tried to be a man of courage in mind as well as body," replied Sternrider. "War is more than piling up mountains of dead bodies. I am the friend as well as the fieldmarshal of your uncle Seaspear and we are well agreed upon our aims of peace and self-protection for both sides in the future."

Then Britania replied, "You talk of peace but all your acts are stabs of cruel warfare. Your king and queen have never offered us a chance of peace."

"You are right, I do agree," replied Sternrider. "And that is why I wish to offer you a deal between the two of us. I cannot speak for Snakeknife or Warchariot. They are ruthless and rapacious as you say but all men fear them for they seized control of the Eagles by deception and illusion.

"They still practice strange arts and consult with witches. Let us ignore them and make a secret bargain between ourselves. Let us be comrades for a future day when Snakeknife and Warchariot will be gone. We should agree that we will never stab our sword against each other for if we warred in face-to-face combat, we both would surely perish.

"When I raise my sword against you, I will cry in triumph and you will run away. I will not follow."

At these words the crias swooped and yelled in anger.

Sternrider continued, "I will not storm your fastness and you will live under my guarantee of peace and safety until you gather together your great armies and move against Warchariot and Snakeknife. This should not be seen as empty theatre or they might overrule my treaty terms. I do believe that they would burn you out. Naturally, I must invade the inland horsemoor regions of your land. You can be sure that I will never kill your horses – that was cruelty. Nor will I move against your harbors or your fleet of ships. For who knows when your four fieldmarshals will return with all their crack divisions?"

"I cannot do this, Sternrider," said Britania. "You need to know that I have never fled before a foe but I believe that this would be the right time for me to do a deal for amnesty."

"Look, Britania, this pact is not a deal – it is a double deal, for I will do the same for you. You will draw your sword and yell 'Retreat' and I will flee with all my men when one day we will meet in the final battle. You are well known as a hero who is fearless but the first task of a champion is to win. Retreat before me now and in return I will flee before you when the last fight roars around us. You owe it to your men to make this pact."

Then she remembered the wise words of Truthteller who had once said, 'Wars are not won only by dealing death but also by alliances and pacts.' She knew that she was tired and weakened by all her fighting, though the Sternrider knew nothing of this.

She snapped her sword more tightly in its sheath and bowed and shook the hand of Sternrider, "Your offer promises a lot for little. I will expect to see you on the day of final reckoning for that last day will surely come and I will claim the victory."

Then Sternrider shook her hand and briefly bowed, "This pact will bring me trouble on that last day but better then than now and I have been in trouble many times before and I have always found escape. You have my word and bond that I will lead the last retreat as I have promised you."

Sternrider drew his sword and yelled, "Retreat."

Britania climbed into her chariot and fled before Sternrider and then she fortified herself and her servants and accoutrements of war and all their longboats in their harbor.

Sternrider left them on their island castle and swept his armies past their harbor fastness into the high horsemoors and village homes of the farms and fields of the East.

When he returned to the Eagle camp he came before Warchariot and his WarQueen Snakeknife who were in a conference with Seaspear and Winterwarrior.

Sternrider bowed before them and humbly presented his claim of victory. "The Seagull Queen has fled before me and is hiding upon her island fastness. We can rule in all the high lands, farms and fields and moors, in all parts of the East where she no longer rules, where I have freed the land. We have won a nominal victory today. Of course, we can find another warrior, one of us here, to go into her fastness and root her out and kill her."

No one spoke until Snakeknife sneered, "Go back yourself – you said that you would kill her, so keep your word."

"That is not true. I said that I would rout her and so I did and not one man among you or among all these armies has defeated her."

And Warchariot became suspicious of Sternrider, "Remember he who fights and runs away will live to fight again some other day and I do not want her flight," said Warchariot, "I want her head."

Sternrider replied, "Within my hand I grasped the rock of the East. I claim this land in the name of Warchariot. Now and forever that land will be yours and all the machines of war and warriors that live there.

"All this sounds very formal," said Warchariot.

"You have the claim in law for all her lands," said Sternrider.

But Warchariot insisted once again, "I do not want this claim. What do I care for law? I am the law. Go back and get her head."

Seaspear spoke to the king, "You said that you would take what you could get from Britania – you have the victory. Let that be enough."

Winterwarrior agreed with the others, "A win is everything."

But Snakeknife persisted, "You must go back and finish her. It will be easy now that she has been defeated. She is probably sick and wounded, weak at the knees no doubt after her turmoils."

Sternrider spoke once more, "My final word is this, no one but me has put the Wavewarrior Queen to flight. Of all our heroes who have died trying, no warrior has defeated her and no one else but me has even come close. I will not go even one more time to fight her, I swear, until my turn comes round again."

So the armies of Sternrider swept into the remote parts of the East avoiding the coastal fringes where the harbors lay.

Queen Snakeknife had her own secret plans and ordered the sub-commanders under the rank of fieldmarshal to seek out signs of seamen. They were to look for symbols or ships or parts of boats and chariots, fishing nets or harpoons or the like. For not all seamen live nearby the harbors. They should put the seamen clans to death at once to make sure they could never use their boats to strike against the Eagles in the future.

This was despite the best peace efforts of Seaspear, the overall fieldmarshal of both fleets. For Seaspear failed to keep his trust and promise that all his seamen would be well protected from the cruel ravages and winds of war.

The Eagle Warriors slashed and cut both farms and homes, burning the barns and food stores to the ground. And old men, retired and resting from their many years of battle, sighed and shook their heads in shame, looking upon the ashes of their homes. Watching the kidnapping of their young grandchildren they muttered bitterly among themselves, "What have we now to lose but our old bones? Let us throw one last stab at these Eagles."

Another spoke, "Let us first hide away the Great White Stallion and his small herd of war horses. We know where they are stamping on the nearby moors. Now we can take them to the secret caves against the day when our young champions and heroes return."

And this was done. Then the old men climbed aboard the creaking chariots with their rusty swords and their broken shields and scabbards. Clutching their javelins and blunt old swords they flung themselves upon the invaders. Like ghosts returning to their past scenes of battle, these sad men were like a legion from the tombs, with the Grim Reaper leading the charge against a startled foe who never expected to die before these former heroes.

On that day, the old Seagull heroes slaughtered many more than three times their own number before they fell upon the sands of combat.

But when Warchariot came upon the scene of battle and saw his slaughtered Eagle Warriors scattered around like food for crows and buzzards he and Snakeknife called for Sternrider, "Send us Seaspear," they told their fieldmarshal. "We will get him to fight the young WarQueen of the Wavewarriors and Seagulls."

***

In the dead of night Sternrider came to visit Britania to tell her to expect Seaspear in single combat and along with him came Gentleleaf, the Queen of Seaspear.

Britania cried, "But Seaspear is my uncle."

"Nevertheless, Warchariot and Queen Snakeknife have consulted with the four witches of kill again and they have somehow persuaded Seaspear to stand and fight against you. Seaspear is bound in honor to protect the seamen of his former fleet. Snakeknife has told him that every day many seamen are dying as long as Britania keeps the war alive. She tells Seaspear he has abandoned those who trusted him – like the dead Queen of Justice – whom you killed. Seaspear is sad and broken but he sees no other way to clear his name and honor."

Britania replied, "But we all implored him not to ally with Warchariot and Snakeknife, even to protect his seamen and his former fleet. There is no such thing as an honorable war. War is the place where truth and honor die with split alliances and hollow promises."

And Gentleleaf, the loyal Queen of Seaspear, pleaded with Britania, "Do not go out – for if two great warriors of the Seagulls should ever combat, one of you must die."

Britania replied, "I have run away one time already and if I did so twice I would lose my kingdom first and then my head. It is impossible. You must tell Seaspear that he should abandon Snakeknife and Warchariot and return to the Seagulls where he belongs."

Gentleleaf wept, "I have begged and pleaded with Seaspear to do so but he is adamant that he must kill you and so avenge his honor."

Then Sternrider shook hands with Britania, climbed back into his chariot and left. Gentleleaf also climbed into her chariot and drove off alongside him back to the Eagle camp. When they returned to the camp they received many side glances of suspicion.

So Seaspear moved his camp to the great straits and told his servants to lay out his arms and all his old accoutrements of war. They did so in silence and in sorrow for they were Seagulls. They knew that they would lose one of their champions of war because of the machinations of Snakeknife.

When Britania had thought about what Seaspear had done she decided that he was treacherous. He had deserted the Seagulls and gone over to the side of their enemy the Eagles and their King Warchariot and his WarQueen Snakeknife.

So when the day of combat came, at the first screech of dawn, she rose up and as she drew near to the straits she saw there was no hint of a greeting from Seaspear. Rather, he seemed withdrawn, silent and brooding within himself.

Britania remembered that Seaspear was no longer a Seagull so she told her servants, "Do not feel sorry for him. He has deserted us and is now one of them – our enemy - an Eagle Warrior."

But as she watched him standing there she was seized with a great sadness and sympathy for Seaspear and she shouted out, "I pray you, my uncle, walk away from this and sail your ships once more among the Wavewarriors."

Seaspear shook his head, still stunned and glassy, "It is too late to walk away, we must fight to the death then one of us may walk when honor has been settled."

So Seaspear called for his extra body armor and skins, his plates of iron as protection against the Bonespear of WarQueen Britania. This was the spear that thirsted for human blood and never failed to find it. Such was its thirst for blood that the Bonespear had to be soaked in red wine daily.

When Britania heard Seaspear ask for this armor, she told her servants, "Hold the Bonespear ready to use, if I should ask for it as a last resort."

Then Seaspear urged his small charioteer to sit well forward between the horses while he drove fierce as a storm towards Britania.

Likewise the young WarQueen Britania urged her chariot forward and both sides clashed together in the strait, parting the low ebb waters in the middle so that the foam flew high into the air and the rocky bottom of the sea lay clear. Both warriors rained great blows upon each other with axe and hammer and broadsword and spear. The demons of the weapons screamed in hatred – even their shields were battered into scrap. But neither won the victory.

At last the quivering javelin of Seaspear found a small crack in the armor of Britania - a slit to let in death. It struck. The blood flowed from the wound like a thin river that colored red the flowing tide of sea.

As Britania weakened, she cried out in desperation, "Throw me the Bonespear now."

She caught the Bonespear in the air and turned it round and drove it through the body of Seaspear as he stood upon his chariot. The Bonespear, made from the dead bodies of heroes, forged in the storms of sea, could never fail. It drove through all the layers of hide and chain and iron plates and sank deep into Seaspear as it reached out greedily for the blood of champions.

Seaspear gasped and sank upon his knees. Feeling the Bonespear eat into his heart and thirstily drink his blood, he cried to Britania, "The pain is over – it is the end. Lend me your sword one last time."

Britania turned the sharp blade of the sword towards her own heart, in an unspoken invitation that said, 'Let us both die at once, for war is futile.'

Then she offered the sword hilt to Seaspear, who smiled and shook his head, "The way is long and hard – not short and easy." Seaspear grasped hard on the hilt of the broadsword of Britania then leaned on one elbow. He swung the sword and cut off his left hand. Seizing the bloody hand, he threw it far onto the eastern shore and said, "That's where my heart and hand will live forever, at least in the remembrance of my combat."

Britania shook her head, "That was not needed. I gladly would have carried you to that shore."

So despite the deep and painful javelin wound she lifted up Seaspear and carried him and laid him on the eastern shore where he would sleep with all his fellow Seagull Warriors and not on the western shore with the cunning Eagles. There the young Britania left her uncle Seaspear gently sleeping beside his red and severed cold left hand.

Then a gloom, a sigh of despair fell upon the Seagulls as their young WarQueen Britania lay wounded.

And Gentleleaf went to the side of the slain Seaspear and mourned for him and placed him in her chariot to take him to the castle of Wavewarriors. There she set him up in his accoutrements of war and armor, mail and helmet, sword, shield and weapons and then placed him upon the prow of his best warship. The ship was set on fire and steered West to sail to the Islands of the Everyoung, there to be mourned by the weeping breezes from the East, with howls from the ghosts of long-gone drowned sailors. And hawks flew up around the burial ship to represent the past triumphs of Seaspear.

Queen Gentleleaf lamented, "He was a pillar of peace and quiet stability and yet a lion for fierceness when he stood against the foe. Seamen and brave Seagull Warriors served him and paid him homage, for they trusted him. He was a fieldmarshal who loved his men but the treachery and cunning machinations of Snakeknife trapped him in the dread grip of honor that destroys. There is no life for me after this loss. There is no vengeance more for me to find – Seaspear was the victim of his honor – I have no love for any man alive. My life can only bring me pain and sorrow."

Then Gentleleaf put her mouth to Seaspear's mouth and put her arms around his neck and sailed far into the western ocean on the ship that glowed and crackled in the pale sunset.

*****

CHAPTER EIGHT

The Fieldmarshals Return

As the Seagull Warriors fell into despair for lack of hope they thought of their four fieldmarshals. The remnants of the Wavewarrior army began to wonder why all their champions and heroes had not returned. So they told Britania that it seemed clear to them that their four fieldmarshals and their champions were being held prisoner by some kind of illusion caused by the witches who worked for the evil WarQueen Snakeknife.

Britania agreed and took herself apart to pray for wisdom. After some hours she came back to their presence and informed them of what she had determined to do.

"Truthteller does not normally interfere in the life of man but I have got permission from him. For there is a pathway of the mind known as the landscape of visions and dreams where any mind may walk to visit another outside the barriers of time and space. I will go there tonight when I sleep and warn our heroes and champions that they are in danger in the Isles of the Everyoung because of the delusions of the witches of kill. I will urge them to return home at once. We need their help."

After a night of deep sleep, the four fieldmarshals in the Isles of the Everyoung awoke the next day to realize that they and all their champions had been deceived. They drank the white wine of clear vision and ate the salmon of wisdom.

They were angry that they had been deluded into leaving the Seagulls helpless without the benefit of their Wavewarrior heroes. At once they ordered their men to seize their arms and all their accoutrements of war to make ready their ships and prepare to sail back home.

Then the Seamaster, one of the immortals, shook his green cloak between the Isles of the Everyoung with their warm jungle trees and fortified harbors so that the Wavewarriors would forget their long exile.

And Stormleaper came to Tear his companion in the Isles of the Everyoung, "As you know there are times in the night when dreams rise up before me in dim vision, scenes of the oldtimes, so I must go."

And Whaleroarer came to Sigh and bid farewell, "I am a warrior and I would be a coward if I remained here when I should be fighting." Sigh gave to Whaleroarer a strong drink of forgetfulness so that he would never hold any memory of her.

Then she said him, "This drink will set you free forever. Truly men seek for what they do not have and what they have seems less than nothing to them."

And Icedragon also said goodbye and sailed from Smile and the Seamaster shook his cloak between them so that they would never meet again.

Likewise, Summersailor came to Laugh and told her, "I am a fieldmarshal and I need to wage a war. I must sail on the tide." But Laugh replied, "I am also a warriorwoman, trained and skilled. I will come with you and help you to fight the battle that has subtler plots and plans." And Summersailor agreed and they sailed away. Yet he remembered nothing of the Isles of the Everyoung.

Following her clear dreamcalls, the young Britania was taking the air and sun high on the ramparts to watch for her fieldmarshals and all their heroes sail into the harbors once more. She began to recall her night dreams and thought about what they had meant.

The first time that I surveyed the heroes who were returning home, I saw that all the small animals had left the plains and shrubberies and taken to the hills.

The second time I saw a thick sea mist float from the ocean so that it made the tops of hills seem to be islands poking out of a lake of mist and fog. Then I saw sparks of fire in this great mist crackling and flaming and flaring from the sea. Then I saw lightning and heard thunder claps and rending and tearing as of sheets of sail and felt a fierce wind blowing from the sea that almost blew me over the side of the rampart.

Those must be the battalions of the four fieldmarshals who have returned by boat and caused the animals to flee to high ground. The thick mist that floated in from the sea was the hot breath of the warriors keen for combat. This was the fog that made the hills seem like islands and the lightnings and the thunders and flames was the flashing of the fierce eyes of the warriors. The enemy will never stand before them.

***

When the four witches of kill heard of the sailings of the fieldmarshals of the Wavewarriors and their heroes they warned King Warchariot and his evil WarQueen Snakeknife that their hostage, Whitehair, was secured and surrounded deep in the witches castle.

"Let them march on you and she will be lost and one of the witches brains will be transplanted. See that the young Britania will be warned and makes no move to jeopardize the life of Whitehair."

So Sternrider sent a message to Britania, "Let us have a time of truce and armistice before you advance your troops against the Eagles. Queen Snakeknife, King Warchariot and the four witches hold Whitehair as hostage and they may destroy her either in body or in mind or both if they so wish."

Britania thought about this for some time and then decided to hold back her warriors for now but instead let her younger brother Stormbolt lead a small party to rescue Whitehair. This would not seem like an overwhelming threat upon the witches. But yet Stormbolt could use strange powers given to him by the Truthteller and may be able to make a small strike upon them without arousing their full fear and vengeance.

And so she sent back word to Sternrider, "Thanks for the warning. I will hold my army for now. I have ruled that only my young brother Stormbolt can rescue her from where she lies in chains in their castle."

So Stormbolt, along with a few stalwart Seagull Warriors, stormed on the mighty army of the Eagles but made no impact. They were scorned and laughed at like a swarm of bees against a rock-built wall. The witches gleed and chortled at the sight.

Outside the domed dungeon of the witches, the rescue party rested and observed the solid castle steeped in arms and magic. They pointed their spears and swords towards the windows and towards the castle doors and drawbridges.

Inside the castle of the four vile witches, Whitehair lay stretched out on the couch beside a great roaring fire that lit the palace and where the smoke drifted up through the open skylight. She was bound both hand and foot and her mouth was gagged but her eyes were watching upwards. She groaned and shook her head and she looked up as the fire and flames swirled up and roared beside her.

Suddenly she saw Stormbolt among the flames. His face was at the smokehole cut in the round-domed castle of the witches. A stunned, short silence fell upon the Eagle army as muttering and confusion came upon them.

Then Stormbolt flew down through the smoke and landed just beside Whitehair, seizing her. He put her underneath his strong left arm and taking shield and weapon in his right hand he jumped and flew up through the smoke and sparks, carrying her through the smokehole of the dome. He flew far over the sea to the castle of the Wavewarriors for he had been given some special powers from the Truthteller.

A great uproar went up from the Eagle army, who had expected only a ground attack. His small rescue party looked up and when they saw Stormbolt and Whitehair change in the air into the form of yellow swans, they stretched their wings and necks and flew away with them into the red sunset.

Now that Whitehair had been rescued and was no longer a hostage, the armies of the Wavewarriors were set free to throw themselves upon the Eagles. Then clash fell upon clash and weaponthunder as the demons of the swords and spears of the Seagulls screamed out for murder, bones and fierce revenge.

But Warchariot rallied his troops and steadied them telling the captains, "Hold your broadswords ready not for the foe but for your men who weaken. If I see any captain who has not killed, for cowardice, at least one of our own men, I swear I will kill that captain on the spot, cutting his head off like freshcaught fish. So the Eagles fought hard against the Seagulls. The two sides fought like an entangled forest and neither side was fit to gain the victory.

When Britania and Sternrider came face to face, as they had done before, she remembered the Truthteller and his advice to make a deal for victory with any one of the enemy who was honorable.

Then the vision and the memory of Sternrider rose before her and she repeated the grim words that Sternrider had promised when they had made a deal, "Retreat before me now and I will flee before you when the last fight roars around us.

"So let this be so and flee from me and my Wavewarriors will not pursue your Eagles but rather we will let you all escape the keen swords of turmoil and vengeance."

Sternrider turned and fled and called on his warriors to escape the cruel yoke of Warchariot and flee to a safe place. "Come let us move aside and give the field to Britania to fight the treacherous killers that your King Warchariot calls captains."

And the forces of the Wavewarriors swept through as the Eagles lines broke. Only Warchariot and his heroes fought a dogged losing battle but the Sternrider set apart his battalions on an island off the south side of the west bank and held it, surrounded by his champions and heroes, as strong as any fastness in the world. And there they held the Great Bay Stallion, much to the grievance of Queen Snakeknife.

The Seagull Warriors of the young WarQueen Britania surrounded but did not invade Sternrider's island and soon they claimed the victory and rode their chariots back with spoils of battle.

***

The Eagles crept impoverished into the woods, the crevasses and caverns of the shadowlands. Like hawks arising over the battlefield was the victory of Britania and the Wavewarriors over Warchariot and his poisonous assassin Queen Snakeknife. For these two were now lurking in holes and watercaves to plot and plan revenge on their fieldmarshal Sternrider. For it was clear to them that he had helped Britania and her Wavewarriors attack the Eagles and win a great victory.

At first Snakeknife and Warchariot laid low, hiding in their remote fastness but later they sought the plots of the four witches of kill. The witches worked in secret, far from Britania and her protection of the exiled Eagles who had changed sides and fought alongside Sternrider.

The witches gathered around to once again use their spells and strange aromas of mindmadness and delusions drawn from the very pit of demons.

Meteoreyes reminded the others that Sternrider had changed allegiances and fights for Britania, "We must destroy our new-found enemy. Let us sharpen and make keen our deadliest poison smeared on the knives and swords and javelins so that the slightest touch from the sharp edges will bring instant death."

Then they called on every wisp of leaves and straw and grass and twigs and flowers dying and dead that flew about in the autumn ground and sky. They cried aloud, "Take on the shape of a huge invading army of men and boats floating in from the sea."

So Sternrider saw this vision of a great invading army filling all the landscape with fierce shouting and yelling as smoke and fire burnt on and crackled brightly. The leaves and grass flew up like screaming devils appearing to surround him like a sea of hideous, laughing deathhead foes.

The friends of Sternrider tried to steady him by telling him, "Do not panic. Do not be afraid of these dark fiends. They do not exist and we cannot see them. These shadows cannot harm you. They are not the fierce howls of warfiends and vile assassins but armies raised up in hell only to lure you into mindmadness."

While the four witches continued their attack on the mind of Sternrider, Warchariot and his sly WarQueen Snakeknife quietly crept to the island where their treacherous fieldmarshal was in hiding.

They saw that Sternrider was frozen in dismay. Suddenly Warchariot seized the deadly poisoned spear and threw it at his former fieldmarshal's chest and cried out loud to him, "Your days of false retreats are over."

Immediately the poison from the spear spread thoughout his veins and the once strong fieldmarshal fell. As his soul began to leave his body, the Great Bay Stallion escaped from his corral and fled past Queen Snakeknife, making good his escape to the eastern world over the seas that flow through the great straits.

At once the Bay Stallion roared and neighed and snorted at Oceanhorse, the Great White Stallion of the East. Then Oceanhorse chomped and bowed low and raised his head and mane to meet the challenge of the Bay. So Snakeknife lost her struggle to retain her mascot Stallion.

As Sternrider lay deepwounded near the lake where a Washerwoman had once foretold his fate, he saw a cria dip down towards his head and then a crow flew down and drank the red blood as it flowed away. Then a buzzard and a hawk hovered above and Sternrider smiled a smile. He saw his life and the life of the old King Waterbear's great eastern army summed up in one great picture of a battlefield as the four birds flew around the fallen Eagle.

As he died, his days of youth returned when he was a fierce warrior in the field and the brightness of a true champion flashed all around him as the aura of his herolight returned.

*****

CHAPTER NINE
Bullaxe

Meanwhile, the red sun rose above the eastern sea as the young Britania's eyes were now set upon more fierce combats. She needed to know if she would have the full support of all the Seagull Warriors now that they had returned from the Isles of the Everyoung and fought with her against the Eagles. Warchariot's killers were always ready to strike in treachery with the claws of witches lurking in the background. So the young WarQueen Britania went to visit with her godfather the Truthteller to get more wisdom.

Britania's sword and shield and gleaming javelins shone in the light of the morning dawn like stars of heaven gathering their spears together. Her yellow skin glowed like her shield of bronze; her dark brown eyes like dagger points set deeply in the keen gashes of her face. She was an oriental princess of air and water. Swifter and more spirithaughty and proud, fiercer and more terrifying and owlwise than many an older and more experienced warrior was the searush of Britania's mindfury as she sailed her longboat quickly back to the castle of the Wavewarriors.

Summersailor often secretly mourned the death not only of Waterbear and Springvision but also the death of peace and order, law and succession among the Seagulls as they argued among themselves as to who should succeed the old King Waterbear.

For many would not accept the young WarQueen Britania and some argued to await the coming of age of her younger brother Stormbolt and some argued for their experienced fieldmarshal Summersailor, the brother of King Waterbear.

Many fine champions came to the Seagull Castle in the hope of setting themselves above the rest or at least finding a high and preferred place with their leader, whoever that might be.

In the vast champion's palace there were rooms for a hundred warriors and their lovely queens. In the great hall the throne was red but empty. Each fine apartment was paneled in red yew; red for the blood that bought the hall for freedom. Along the walls were javelins, shields and swords twinkling like stars of gold. The silver glimmered on the necks and coils of copper javelins, on the rims of mighty shields, on the chalices and goblets and the drinking horns.

Servants and attendants, cooks and wine bearers, tables and chairs and couches filled the palace. Behind the empty throne stood heads and trophies, weapons and jewels and finest pins and broaches, of enemies long past and dead forever.

Beside the throne, for privacy in the making of royal commands, stood mighty screens of copper. These screens were all decked with gold and silver birds whose eyes were jewels, picked out and polished and long traveled from all over the world. These were the whispering screens of kingly secrets.

Gradually a gray mist dropped like a pall upon the palace. Underneath the mist a festering swamp rose up out of the earth with sharp foul smells.

Out of the swamp there strode an ugly oaf, a huge man, fat of mouth, heavy of shoulder, panting and puffing like a buffalo. His eyes were baggy and his face was bristling with sharp gray stubble and thick bushy eyebrows. His face was well wrinkled with thick hanging skin and on his head, dark short-cropped patchy hair. His teeth were blunt, black, misshapen and uneven.

As the Wavewarriors gathered in the palace, the oaf's footsteps made the earth to quake and quiver and the trophies shook on the wall, trembling and jingling.

The monster clomped and lumbered slowly and clumsily in his green leathery shoes as he entered the hall before the great assembly. He slouched forward, eight feet tall with a thick neck and head. His eyes bulged out and his flat nose was snorting like a great bull, dressed up in human guise. His arms and legs were caked with soil. He carried across his arms a huge and gleaming axe as long as any warrior. The blade was four feet in breadth, curved and sharp, keen as a razor.

The smell that hung around his body was like that of weeds from an old heap of dung or from flowers and bushes that hung around his head or from his coat of tree's bark, leaves and branches. On his sleeve were the yellow and green cuffs of an oaf.

"I am Bullaxe," he roared. "I have come to this assembly of champions who would be king or queen to test if any one man can be found to keep his word. One man of skill and courage is all I ask. I have searched the world and never can I find one man of courage with skill and honor.

"All warriors have failed me. I ask because you have need of such good men to be your generals and to be your new WarQueen or King now that the brave Waterbear has been so brutally murdered. You need a man of guts and skill and truth, for who can live with liars and assassins?"

"You have spoken well but who is fit to judge these virtues of a king?" asked

Summersailor, "Who are you Bullaxe to judge?"

The ogre raised his hand, "Silence," he roared. "You all will judge. I bring only a test of fairness, courage and skill. I say, accept my simple challenge, Tit for Tat and Blow for Blow. That's a fair deal and an honest bargain. Let's have it so, a Blow for Blow fair deal. O let's have fun and all can be agreed on This for That - so you do yours and then I will do mine. O we'll have such happy fun."

The company relaxed and many asked "What are these children's games that you propose?"

"O yes, it's fun," the ogre roared, "It's just that I cut off your head tonight, then you come back tomorrow night and cut off mine. You see it's just a test of courage, skill and honor. Let's see if you have the skill to take my head, the courage to face up to me, the honor to come back here tomorrow as agreed so that you in turn can chop off my poor head."

"This is all nonsense, for how can any man keep his appointment when he is dead?" cried Summersailor. "Go back to your black hole you are a fool."

The ogre Bullaxe paused for breath and thought. "Stop. Ha, Ha, I see what you mean. So you go first. Whichever way, it is all right with me. Let any warrior chop off my head tonight. See? Then I will come and chop off his tomorrow. Yes, Tit for Tat is anyway you want it. And Head for Head, my head your head, is fair. So what's the difference in who goes first? Let anyone who would be king or queen go first. Ha, Ha, we'll have such fun and games tonight."

Fireball, an obscure warrior and little known, who was ambitious and impetuous, spoke up to stake his claim upon the championship. "Then I will go first. I will chop off your head right now and you can chop off my head tomorrow."

So Bullaxe cleared a circle before the fire and moved a log into the centre of it, handed his mighty axe over to Fireball and lay face down with his neck upon the log and submissively and mildly closed his eyes. Fireball took hold of the massive axe with difficulty and raised it high above the head of Bullaxe.

The company stood quite still and gasped in horror as Fireball brought down the axe with all his might upon the ogre's neck but did not sever it, achieving only a deep gash upon the side where blood poured out and spurted in a stream.

Some of the ladies were shocked at the sight of the blood. They turned themselves into seagulls and flew up into the rafters, screeching in terror, as Bullaxe rose up and shook his fists at them.

"Small sympathy I get when I am mutilated," he railed at them.

Then he turned to Fireball and seized back his axe from the unconqueror, "Bungler and weakling, you have broken the bargain. You have not cut off my head. Now play the game. Let us be fair and not torment each other."

Bullaxe seized Fireball by the throat and threw him over the log and cut off his head. "Your wound was merely puerile. Cut off my head next time properly, decently and cleanly."

As the blood poured out from the neck of Bullaxe, he cried in a loud voice, "Here is my axe. Let any man take it into his hand.

Will any man be man enough to behead me right now and I will behead him tomorrow night? Accept this simple challenge, Tit for Tat, Head for Head, an honest bargain."

So the Wavewarriors whispered among themselves, "The ogre is insane and who knows what magic he has in mind for us. Who knows who sent him here or for what strange reason? Let us get rid of him and all his hatreds."

Then a Seagull shot an arrowbolt at Bullaxe from a crossbow. Bullaxe seized the bolt like a child swatting a mosquito in the air and threw it back to the bowman, splitting his head and killing him instantly. After that, no one dared to shoot a missile at Bullaxe.

So the ogre ranted, "Quick, do let me die now, please cut off my head and let me cut off yours tomorrow night."

"I say he must be mad," cried out Summersailor, "a renegade of the moon willing to let anyone cut off his head." Summersailor came to the conclusion that Bullaxe really was prepared to die.

His henchmen whispered quietly to Summersailor, "You can take him. If you can get his head he cannot rise to strike again for once he's dead, he's dead. This will be glory for you."

So Summersailor cried out to the ogre. "Calm Bullaxe and forgive us now for allowing only Fireball to play this game with you. He was a quick and courageous warrior but as for skill and strength, not quite the best. Forgive us for not sending out our champion. I am the first fieldmarshal of all Wavewarriors. Next to the young WarQueen Britania, who is not here, I am the supreme one. I will cut off your head tonight and you may cut off mine tomorrow night if that is quite acceptable to you and if you are not too wounded to endure it."

Then Bullaxe laughed loudly. "Me get wounded? What a joke! I like to play my game of Head for Head. It is such fun and fair and elegant."

Whitehair, the niece of Summersailor, stood slender and delicate. She was a young thoughtful lady, pure as a swan and wise as a nightowl. She spoke quietly to her uncle, "Do not do this; this is an evil bargain and steeped in witchcraft. You would do better to ignore his cruel raving. I beg you Uncle, do not play this game. The Tit for Tat of Bullaxe is not fair."

But Summersailor whispered to his niece, "There is no danger. Once he's dead, he's dead."

Whitehair replied, "The wicked never die, they live forever in filthy forests, the home of all ugly spirits. So take care, my uncle."

But Summersailor paid no heed.

Then Bullaxe cleared a circle before the fire and moved a log into the center of it, handed his mighty axe over to Summersailor and lay facedown with his neck upon the log, submissively and smiling, closing his eyes. Summersailor took hold of the massive axe with ease and raised it high above the neck of Bullaxe.

Whitehair drew back and turned her head in horror as Summersailor, with all his might, brought down the axe upon the neck of Bullaxe and severed the head sharply from its body. Some of the ladies shrieked and changed their form into seagulls, flying and fluttering into the rafters high above.

The head of Bullaxe rolled over on the floor and screamed in pain as blood poured out from eyes, ears, nose and mouth and from its severed neck.

In agony, it swore revenge on the Summersailor. "Tomorrow I will repay you for this torment," spat out the head and then began to laugh and chortled, "Ha, Ha, only joking friends. What fun and fairness that will be for me."

Bullaxe stood up and took back his axe from Summersailor then he lifted up his bleeding head from off the floor and clutched it to his chest. The head spoke to Summersailor, "You have great courage for agreeing to my bargain and skill for chopping off my head so cleanly. But do you have the honor and the truth to come back here tomorrow night so that I can chop off your head as we agreed? Tit for Tat and Head for Head."

Summersailor grew faint and dizzy with fear and fell back as the ogre's head spoke out, moaning and bleeding from underneath his arm.

With axe in one hand and his head in the other, with blood still streaming down his chest and falling upon the floor, the ogre turned away and muttered casually, "Bit of a breeze is brewing up tonight perhaps it's one of your wavewarriors from the deep."

The warriors standing by were silent and stood stunned beyond all words with fear and disbelief.

And the severed head of the ogre sneered and winked at the seagulls hiding high in the metamorphoses brought upon them by their terror.

The head sneered, "You will be glorious in days of war to come."

But as he lumbered out of the silvery palace, clutching his head and axe, the head screamed, "Tomorrow night, my turn to behead you, in honesty and integrity and justice - you who would be the commander of the Wavewarriors. Be here and ready great Summersailor, brother of the old King Waterbear. See you keep your word."

Then the Wavewarriors in the Seagull Palace went to their rooms to rest. As the night fell, a great storm from the sea began to brew and waves of salt seawater leapt up high and the wind growled out. A low baritone of thunder grumbled innocently in the far isolated distance. It was just a genteel cough, an incidental cough and a mere clearing of the deep waters throat.

But yet how treacherous, lying and deceitful can a seaweed tempest be? For very soon, small colored creatures fled. Rabbits and foxes, dogs and mice and cats, scurried away from the low-lying fields, along the shore, to creep into the higher ground of trees and caves and bushes in the hills. There to burrow and hide quietly from the storm which now began to stir and roar and flood jungles of sea and land. And Summersailor joined them to hide from Bullaxe and his bargain.

A sharp shout from the fierce sea storm's tongue spread out across the forest hills and slopes in a cold, cold blast as the giant of the deep roared out his grief and imminent revenge.

The next evening, as stormwaters lapped around the palace floors, all the warriors gathered to see if Bullaxe would reappear. But Whitehair eagerly awaited the return of her friend, the young WarQueen Britania.

"Look," cried the watchman from the parapet, "The ogre is returning, clomp upon clomp; he walks like one possessed by anticipation; he stomps here eagerly in search of heads.

"See, he is whole. His head back on his shoulders and his head and neck is unmarked on his body and just as though it never had been severed. As large as life and twice as natural, he lumbers inexorably towards our fortress."

Then the watchman turned into a frightened seagull and flew into the rafters, there to screech. Some warriors closed and barred the great front door.

So Bullaxe appeared once more, kicked down the door and entered. His breath was putrid and his look was mean, nasty, destructive and ugly. He was seeking and searching like a big bully looking for a child to murder.

His arms were thick and muscular and powerful with wiry sinews ready to squeeze out life from any creature. Like a hard and cruel yokel his butt stuck out like a tree trunk well behind him for he was a swaggering, arrogant and audacious, filthy oaf.

Bullaxe peered around at the warriors and sneered and roared aloud, "Step forward Summersailor, it's my turn now. How I am going to enjoy this fun of beheading with the test of fairness, courage and skill. I say, accept my simple challenge – Tit for Tat.

"Where are you Summersailor? Only last night you chopped my head off, now I will enjoy chopping your head off. It is a fair bargain. Oh let's play games Summersailor. Where are you?"

And the ogre held his axe out at the ready but Summersailor was already hiding away in the high hills.

Then Whitehair, the niece of the Summersailor, spoke out. "My uncle is not here nor should he be. You speak of fairness but magic is not fair and you are practicing some kind of magic."

Bullaxe answered, "I am here to set a test of championship - to test and uphold skill and truth and to expose the cowards and liars. No one will ever win who fears to die. And your uncle is a liar and a coward. The people of the Wavewarriors have excelled all other people in power, weaponry and all the arts of battle and in truth, generosity and dignity.

"People all fear you. Can I not find a warrior, even one among you who will keep his word? Where is your family honor and integrity?"

Then Whitehair answered as she pointed her long, slim finger at Bullaxe, "She stands behind you listening to your rant."

The ogre turned and crouched, twitching his axe. "What flotsam has the storm washed up?" he roared and laughed with joy to see the young Britania standing behind him.

There in the open doorway of the palace the ogre saw Britania, armed for battle, her skin a yellow-glowing in the sun. The water and the seaweed dripping from her glittered and glowed among her golden weapons. Although young, she was ready for war. Around her head a hero-light shone and small birds flew in the halo. Aromas, flowers and foliage and seaweed hung in the air; the smells of afterstorm were strong around her. Even the ogre held his breath to see her and stepped back, but not in fear, only in respect and awe.

"What do you want of me?" asked the young Britania.

And Bullaxe answered with a thick stabbing finger, "Your father's brother has not kept his bargain to let me take his head, after he had beheaded me last night. Therefore your clan and all your people are today dishonored by his fear of death. So go your way and join the ranks of cowards to be forgotten, for many are the cowards of this world."

The young Britania answered Bullaxe, "Then let me take the place of my good uncle. May I be sacrificed for family honor and be headcut in place of Summersailor. So you cut off my head, for he has cut off yours, though that has seemed to do you little harm. As you say, cut my head off and avenge yourself in justice or in honest fun and games."

Then Bullaxe laughed and roared in hilarity. "Yes, let me find a fair and honest bargain. When you lie down and I cut off your head, you will be in the place of Summersailor. Naturally, for Fair is Fair and Tit for Tat, then you can take my head off in return."

As Britania lay down with her neck upon the log, submissively and mildly closing her eyes Bullaxe raised his axe above the head of the young Britania. Then he brought it swiftly down with all his might upon the hand of Truthteller who now appeared protecting the young WarQueen Britania.

Whitehair drew back and turned her head in horror but Britania lay there well and whole. The great palace roared a shout of triumph as the young Britania rose up to her feet and bowed to her godfather, the Truthteller, master of good words.

Then Truthteller took his sheaf of crossbow darts and shook those silver bolts ready to shoot them into the heart of any liar.

Bullaxe bowed low to the tall and erect Truthteller and mumbled, "I had no right to take the head of Britania, in place of Summersailor."

Then turning to address the young WarQueen, Bullaxe cried, "You have passed my test in courage and in truth and honor but not in skill and strength. Let's see if you are strong and skilled enough to behead me.

Let's play my little game of Tit for Tat and Head for Head, in turn. For you must pass in skill as well as in guts and truth."

Bullaxe handed his mighty axe to Britania and lay facedown with his neck upon the log and in quiet cheerfulness he closed his eyes. Britania took hold of the massive axe with ease and raised it high above the neck of Bullaxe. Then she severed the head sharply from its body. The head rolled over on the floor and bled great clots of blood from eyes and ears and nose and from its severed throat.

In agony the head of Bullaxe swore vengeance but the young Britania drew her strength and struck the head again until it silenced under the blows and fell into small pieces. The crushing blows of the great axe was like the wind as it cut through branches of great trees, tempest tossed in a might of rattling storm.

Nevertheless, Bullaxe stood up again and gathered the pieces of his head even as they bled and, seizing back his axe, stalked to the doorway laughing and a-murmuring in a deep mutter.

"You have passed, young Britania, in courage and in honor and now in skill," muttered the fragments of the severed head.

Bullaxe strode out of the doorway holding his head, fitted together from its several pieces.

The dignified Truthteller, tall in his eternal strength and power, followed after the Bullaxe. The great Truthteller of the universe, the king of good wisdom, held the true-word bolts for his crossbow as he walked beside the mutilated monster from the swamp that was bleeding and groaning from his cruel beheading.

As they strode away from the great gate of the palace, Truthteller shot a flash of flying darts from his great crossbow, winging across the sky - all deadly shots of truths from his sure hand, piercing the throats of random liars, speaking all over the world and choking them to death.

Then Truthteller flew to his secret home afar off.

The ugly oaf, Bullaxe, plodded on. Still lumbering, he changed back into a bushy treetrunk as he sank into his bog and disappeared.

After they had gone, the young WarQueen Britania was welcomed by the other warriors and by her cousin Whitehair who asked her, "How could you have laid down in the way you did? If Truthteller had not saved you, you would have died. And we would have lost our WarQueen to challenge King Warchariot and his evil WarQueen Snakeknife and all their assassins."

Then Britania took the lovely hand of Whitehair and kissed it, "My dear cousin, if it is my destiny to avenge the death of my father I knew I would not die. If it should not be my destiny, then I would just as soon have died there on that log, as my head rolled, for life would not be good without my honor. Now I am sure that my true destiny is to one day avenge my father's murder and to make a place for many to dwell in peace."

At these words dread fell on the assembly for they knew that horrible wars must soon follow. Many raised up their swords and saluted the young Britania as they proclaimed her the WarQueen of the Seagull Wavewarriors, first in skill, courage and in honor but some were still uneasy with the prospect of a warqueen.

Later, Summersailor came into the palace after talking to some of the Wavewarriors. He bowed his head and addressed his niece Whitehair, "My niece, come with me for we are going over to the army of Warchariot. Icedragon, our great hero, has also decided to join us. You will be safe with us and live in honor with King Warchariot and his owlwise Queen Snakeknife."

"Why should we live under the protection of those two treacherous and devious murderers?" she replied, "Why have you decided to leave us when we really need your leadership?"

And Summersailor bowed his head and thought. Then he raised his head up high and answered her, "Britania's father had a fatal flaw. A king must always be cautious and cunning. Waterbear had no sense of fear. He had no judgment. Your aunt Springvision and I, his brother, warned and begged and pleaded with the Waterbear not to risk his life at the false funeral.

"Waterbear and Springvision are both dead. I fear the fault of acting without judgment will now fall on Britania and it may destroy us all. Remember that she killed Seaspear – rightly or wrongly.

"Britania is young, headstrong and impetuous and her young brother Stormbolt has not yet finished his training in the arts of war with his greatuncle Shadowhero, so there is little to support Britania."

But Whitehair replied to her uncle Summersailor, "You need not fear, for I will remain with her for all she needs now is loyalty and support.

"Anyway, is it such a fearful thing for a warqueen to be brave, headstrong and impetuous? I say, let Britania be just like her father. She has been judged by the oaf Bullaxe to be a woman of courage, skill and honor."

As Summersailor thought upon the words of his niece, Whitehair, many of the Wavewarriors milled round and talked in discontent late into the night.

The birds flew out of the bushes and flocked upwards and the moon dimfaded into the light of dawn as the sun rose up out of the East like a hero. A new day had dawned, led by Britania, WarQueen of the Seagulls, with a fury light shining around her head and a halo of fire and brightness flashing about her. But when Britania was told that two of her fieldmarshals had gone with part of her army, a dark cloud descended on the Wavewarrior Castle.

*****

CHAPTER TEN
Words of Wisdom

At the castle of Warchariot and his WarQueen Snakeknife there was a great uproar as the sound of a mighty army was heard approaching the castle.

Servants rushed up to the parapet and looked across the plains. There in the distance they saw two chariots coming and behind those chariots clouds of dust as of many men and horses. It was a great army of fighting men in chariots with weapons gleaming in the sun coming in the distance.

The company of Wavewarriors were wined and dined as their two fieldmarshals Summersailor and Icedragon went aside to consult with Warchariot and WarQueen Snakeknife.

Summersailor was introduced to the Eagle fieldmarshal Winterwarrior.

"Here meet your opposite from the Eagles," said Warchariot, "the viceking of the hills, Winterwarrior the veteran and fieldmarshal. As you may know, it is our hope to avoid a war of kill. So talk to the great fieldmarshal of all the divisions of the Eagles. Then you can talk man to man of peace and plenty."

Old Winterwarrior was most frank and friendly. He warmly shook the hand of Summersailor.

"It seems you rule the waves and we the land. This we could bear, if we could have free passage to cross the seas but if you block our way how can we avoid a conflict where too many can only lose their lives and limbs and fortunes. Come here with me and I will show you all our secret stores of wealth that could be yours if only you would join us and not murder us."

"I hope this can be so. But your King Warchariot and his Queen Snakeknife were the ones who started all the murder and mayhem," replied Summersailor.

"Yes," Winterwarrior agreed, most pleasantly. "Just so and I am glad you mentioned this. I had no part of that. Warchariot is cold and cruel."

At this point Winterwarrior looked around furtively, "It would be no great hardship for me to be king but I would never dare to move against him. He is too murderous. Also there is no need. One day, and soon, his enemies will destroy him. You might as well be my true righthand man instead of viceking to the young WarQueen Britania.

"And young heroes come and go but we old warriors go on forever. We are time and combat scarred. Anyway Summersailor let me show you something and think about what I said. Here in this basement . . ." (as they came to a large stone flight of steps and entered and passed the ten ranks of guardians and heroes) "is the greatest thing that any army can have - all you will ever need of food and gold.

"And there is a pile of gold, right in the center, as large as three good pigs. My crack division needs a rich supply of living gold and food for fighting, as you can see, in order to keep my men going like heroes and you deserve no less for your Hawkarmy. Where else in all the world could you get this? Here, take a small sample of this gold to test it."

Summersailor lifted up a piece of gold, appraised it, held it up to catch the light, nodded in appreciation and acceptance and put it in his pouch.

Then Winterwarrior, fieldmarshal of the Eagles and Summersailor went back to join the feasting.

While they were talking, the sly Queen Snakeknife had been eavesdropping on the conversation and heard everything but kept it to herself.

The next day Summersailor rose up at the dawn, like a cock that struts at the screech of the day, he siezed his Hardblade Rainbowsword. A herolight shone all about the warrior and a halo of fire and brightness flashed around him as he leapt out to greet his crack division, the best of the Wavewarriors. He gave the cry, "Hawkrise," and they rose up, ready for a demonstration of their skills. Then he unsheathed his Rainbowsword, swung it around and drew a rainbow, high in the sky above. The dawn streaked over the sky in grey and light blue.

Everyone sat up to see the Hawkarmy arising. Winterwarrior, the viceking of the Eagles, did not comment during these exercises but viewed the mock battles with the greatest pleasure.

After the display was over everyone returned to the hall. Summersailor bowed low to Winterwarrior and then he and Icedragon went with Winterwarrior to consult about how to put their two armies together.

***

Meanwhile, the young WarQueen Britania along with her cousin Whitehair and her ladies-in-waiting prayed to the good forces of the universe for true success and wisdom as a queen.

Later the young Britania and the other ladies sat high on the roof of the fastness where they were joined by Whaleroarer and Stormleaper.

But even now they were still not sure of the true fate of Icedragon or Summersailor. They wondered if they had become deserters or had gone as spies for the Wavewarriors.

So Britania spoke to the others, "I need true wisdom. So now I ask of each of you a saying, a word of guidance as a gift to me to set me on the right path. My enemies will not hear."

Then Stormleaper bowed, "I pledge my loyalty to you. My word of wisdom is: Set right the wrongs of those who are oppressed. Be just to friend or foe. Take up the cause of the good poor against the wicked rich. Do not let prejudice or passion rule. Be cold and sharp in judgments; in short – be fair."

Likewise, the huge Whaleroarer also pledged his loyalty, "I give you all my help Britania. My word of wisdom is: Do not be rash. Do not take part in drinking feasts. Do not make threats, only fulfill them. Do not set aside good advice because the adviser is poor or old and do not take advice because the adviser is rich. Think about all ideas, for that is the calmness and dignity of a queen. Do not make foes except for a good reason. Do not always try to be first or best.

"Do not hold lotteries or any idle competitions. In that way, for every winner there must be created dozens of losers. Only a few winners can take the prize but many will be losers and weep in disappointment. Avoid debt. For this presumes that funds will always be available to pay in future – this will not always be so. Keep clear of dirty tricks of winning and losing. Do not be arrogant. Do not be boastful. Do not speak noisily. Above all be cautious."

Then the beautiful warriorwoman Streamflower knelt down before the young warqueen and bowed.

"I will pray for you Britania. I will pray to the universal power of good. I will pray that you may come to understand the things that the powers of good want you to do and pray that you will summon up the courage to do them without the fear of man. Above all, pray."

Then Maplewine knelt down before the queen. "Britania, I will read to you or sing when you are pondering about deep problems. So read and listen and study to be wise and so you will build reserves of strength and power. Read only the good books, long read of old and deeply revered by all. Life is too short to read the frivolous. Above all, plan."

Then Maplewine bowed low to the young Britania who smiled and thanked the girl.

And Willowflame also bowed to Britania, her red hair like a burning willow tree.

"This is my tribute of a word of wisdom: Do not take gifts to do the unjust thing. If you do make mistakes take the blame squarely. Do not take what is not yours because of your position. Restore all things to those who have been robbed.

"Only with good cause grant favors or refuse them. In dealing war, put to death no one because of his poverty and spare the life of no one because of his riches. Do protect from thieves. Above all, be honest."

The young warqueen thanked the girl, bright Willowflame.

Then Britania turned to her cousin Whitehair, "My loyal friend, give me your word of wisdom."

Whitehair truly advised Britania, "Do not give out and do not listen to false, idle talks or wicked tittle tattle and rather test the gossip with good questions to find the truth, for truth is all in all. Be kind and loyal to ladies and to friends for we are utterly dependent on you. Do not punish a fool who does not know what he is doing. Do not demand more of any person than he can do with honesty. Do not be a jester or a joker for that is not becoming to a ruler of men. Be serious and thoughtful and be true."

Then Britania thanked them all for their words of wisdom and said, "Here is my word of wisdom to you all. There are only two forces in the universe, Builders or Breakers: that is Do or Undo: Make or Break. Swords of sun or daggers of night. The eternal powers of good or ill.

"See that you serve only the spirits of good for every deed that you carry out and every thought that you even think will bounce off the far wall of the universe, where it is multiplied at least ten-fold and comes straight back to hit you in body and spirit so that you will reap ten times what you did sow of good or ill. May good works flow to you. And so I say to you, above all, do good."

Then Britania, the new WarQueen of the Wavewarriors sat by herself high on her fastness overlooking the sea and considered the many words of wisdom from her fieldmarshals and their warqueens.

***

As time went by she sent out brightly colored birds that bore a message to her distant islands. "Come to us now for we need your help to build up our fleet against the cruel armies of our enemies, the Eagles. They are gathering up their arms and accoutrements of war to destroy us. Sail to us speedily for we have been disrupted with warwords and all our ships and heroes have been turmoiled. Sail to our lough with all your ships and seamen."

The small talking birds flew far, far away to speak this message to the scattered Seagulls. For nine long days Britania pondered what to do when suddenly she saw a fleet of ships on the horizon. She took the form of a yellow, widewinged seabird and flew over the fleet to find out whether they were friends come to support her or enemies.

Britania spread her wings over the fleet and blackened out the sun. Then a savage storm arose in the sky below her wings and the dark clouds brooded slowly over the sea.

The fleet cringed below Britania's wings, as the winds brewed and the waves leapt high in fear and mermaids screamed as their hair streamed out in terror. The small birds and the seagulls screeched in madness and the green seaweeded waves were in an uproar as the cold waters stirred in anger.

The birds that hovered overhead were insane as they attacked each other and threw themselves upon the barks and boats. The ropes all strained and stretched and the woods of the boats groaned.

The crossbeams creaked and the sails ripped in the rain. The masts shivered and cried and tore in two as the shadow of Britania fell upon them. The ribs of many ships were battered and broken. The gear swept overboard as men clung to the sides. Even the nails in the woods withered and shuddered and some of the sailing craft were overturned as the hulls of the boats swept floating over the masts. The nearby rocks moaned and wept in the bitter blasts.

But Britania saw no foe among the fleet and folded her great wings like an albatross and glided to the shore of her own island.

The storm grew calm with the blue waves lapping mildly. The winds grew tame like birds within their nests and the seas flowed gently by coves and rocks and harbor.

Then the sea became a friendly tide of passage once more as the great fleet came ashore in shouts of triumph. No one had need to row or sail in turmoil as their sails filled out with the warm winds of travel as the sea led them ashore to join their new WarQueen Britania.

The first boat was filled with ugly men of war with close-cropped hair, faces of warts and scars. Loudmouthed they were, sweating, hard-bodied and fierce as they were heard yelling for the blood of Warchariot and his WarQueen Snakeknife. They spat and cursed and cried, Revenge for brave Waterbear.

The largest of the longboats held a champion, for at its prow stood the bravest of the brave. A herolight shone all about that warrior. A halo of fire and brightness flashed around him.

WarQueen Britania stood on the ramparts and cried out to her ladies, "See in that prow there stands a straight and tall man. His cheeks are red as blood, his skin is yellow, his brows are gray, his eyes gray-blue. His hair is long and wavy, white as snow. His frown is like the snarling of a tiger. Heart of stone! That is the Icedragon come back."

The Icedragon strode ashore to shouts of joy from those who loved his coming.

Britania welcomed this hero, "I thank you Icedragon for these men and ships. We need you and we need these tough sea fighters who all have now survived a short storm trial."

The Icedragon replied, "I scanned the seas and I led away as many as would follow. So, here are 200 ships all filled and furious with rebels against Warchariot and his evil WarQueen Snakeknife."

Later Britania took her throne on the high roof and looked out at the longboats of Icedragon, for the ships had been hauled ashore to be fixed and fitted, armed and redecked and roped like a fleet of war.

Around the ramparts sat the heroes, Icedragon, Whaleroarer and Stormleaper. In the centre on pillows of seabirds' down and woolen cushions, sat Britania with her cousin Whitehair and her ladies-in-waiting.

Then Icedragon told of his adventures since he had gone away to the castle of Warchariot and Snakeknife with the restless Summersailor.

"When Summersailor invited me to join him, I refused but offered to go with the Hawkarmy to train and protect them. I asked Summersailor for his sure guarantee of my neutrality. He gave me this protection in the hope that I would change my mind and join him later.

"However, such strange events and sights and such dark omens took place that Summersailor almost led the Hawks back to our side but he did not do so or lead them from the weird killers of the Eagles.

"When I followed Summersailor to the castle of the Warchariot and his WarQueen Snakeknife I saw and met the cruelest murderers of the Eagles. These are the ones who kill by various means of treachery and poison.

"They have some powerful battle heroes too but most are those who kill by cunning and go out into the world as hired assassins.

"In the fastness of Warchariot and Snakeknife, where your brave earthly father was lured and killed, I saw a clan of murderous disguisers. They were all skilled in dressing to look like their prey."

As Icedragon continued to describe in details all the evil he saw at the castle of Warchariot and his WarQueen Snakeknife, they were all distressed and stunned to hear of the horrors that were lying in wait there.

Britania thanked Icedragon, "You have risked your life to tell us about these horrors that we must confront one day soon. Now, tell us about Warchariot and his evil WarQueen Snakeknife, what are their minds focused on now and how do you think they will attack us?"

Icedragon shook his head and then thoughtfully replied, "Warchariot's sick mind is near to confusion. When I came to him at first he and his WarQueen Snakeknife along with their fieldmarshal Winterwarrior were very glad to have us join them. But later he did not welcome any of us but rather sent out for soothsayers, interpreters of signs, readers of omens and the like, to guide him.

"A redrobed young girl had ridden up in her chariot. She was red-skinned with three red pupils in each eye and had the gift of sure foresight.

"Under our very faces, Warchariot asked her to prophesy whether we would help or hinder in his war. He skulked and plucked his beard and scratched his face and scrutinized us. He peered at us suspiciously.

"Pointing at me and Summersailor he asked the visionary, what did she see of Icedragon the hero or Summersailor the fieldmarshal, the two generals just come to join his army and to guide him.

"The young girl told him that she saw blood upon them.

"Then Snakeknife cried out, 'Of course, in a great battle the blood of enemies will splatter on our men, even on us and accidents will happen. We may even wound each other by mistake but we will win, look at our future.'

"The girl in red replied, 'I see blood on you. I see blood on your captains and your warriors. I see the crows fly down to drink your blood and wild dogs crunching on your bones.'

"Then Summersailor spoke, 'My swift Hawkarmy was the crack division of Britania's hosts. Hear the mighty army of the Wavewarriors approaching like the seagulls of the sky, in winds of winter, to join us."

"The redwoman cracked her whip and drove off calmly, 'I see blood, Summersailor. I see blood,' she cried as she rode off.

"Snakeknife was furious and raised her spear, 'I can still transfix her.'

" 'Do not,' Warchariot told her, 'our omens are bad so let us take this warning to improve them. Killing a wise one, a strange prophetess, might bring bad luck and only make things worse. Let us be calm and think what we must do.'

"Then the king's juggler threw up seven swords and seven apples, passing each other like bees on a summer day. The sword would cut the apples in mid-air and the apples would be caught by the juggler before they hit the ground, but now all fell upon the ground and smashed into pieces.

"Warchariot asked, 'Why now for the first time in forty years has this trick failed to work? I feel the evil eye lurking all around us.'

"Then the crows and the ravens screeched and cawed loudly in the battlements. Wild ghosts in the walls yelled out and laughed and uproared. Crocodiles ground their teeth and croaked and grinned in the filthy moats that kept the foe at bay. The stone flags of the castle shook and shifted.

" 'What is that powerful roar?' said WarQueen Snakeknife as she jumped up to her feet.

"Then Warchariot drew his sword and grasped his javelin.

" 'This is my gift to you,' laughed the Winterwarrior.

" 'What kind of gift would make this castle shudder?' asked Warchariot.

"Snakeknife cried out, 'Is this some kind of joke?'

"Winterwarrior pointed his hand at the Summersailor, 'That mighty roar is the Summersailor's Hawks, the crack division of the Seagull Warriors.'

" 'No,' said Snakeknife, 'an army out of nowhere? I see you are laughing. Do not make fools of us. Surely the great seamonster that holds up the seabed has turned over on its back and split the seaswamps into seething earthquakes.'

"King Warchariot sprang outside to see the cause. Thousands of birds had landed all around the castle. Perched on rocks and sand, the white screeching seahawks were jumping up and down and fluttering their wings.

"Then hazily they changed into fierce warriors and war horses and chariots of battle.

"Warchariot, pleased with the new Hawkarmy, cried out, 'Each warrior fights like a hardened, seasoned fighter. He knows what he needs to do and how to do it.'

"But WarQueen Snakeknife fumed with jealousy and resentment, 'It would be foolish to accept these Hawks. They would get all the credit for our victories and our own warriors would be driven to a mutiny. The Hawks would get all spoils and again our men would get but little and hate us and desert us. Let us leave these Hawks behind. I do not trust them.'

"Then fieldmarshal Winterwarrior spoke up to defend the great warriors of the Hawkarmy that had joined him, 'But they are fighting for us. If we reject them they will go and fight for the other side. They might even try to seize our land when we had gone and turned our backs on them, to go to war.' Then he bowed to Warchariot.

"It was clear that Warchariot agreed with Winterwarrior but his WarQueen Snakeknife still objected, 'Let us put our own commanders over them to rule them.'

"Warchariot shook his head, 'They would not follow anyone but a leader sanctioned by the Summersailor, their feared fieldmarshal.'

"Snakeknife was obsessed with jealousy and cried out, 'Then let us kill them swiftly unawares. See how our archers line up on the ramparts with their arrows pointed down at this Hawkarmy. We have the advantage over them. Let us just kill them. Thus, we will never need to fight them.'

"Summersailor jumped up and pointed his finger at the Snakeknife, Queen of the

Assassins. 'You will do this only over my dead body.'

" 'That is the general idea,' said WarQueen Snakeknife, grimly.

" 'That may not be so easy,' replied Summersailor.

"Warchariot tried to calm the stirring waters. 'We are not strong enough to kill them, nor can we just send them off to help the enemy,' Warchariot had muttered.

"Snakeknife sneered in hatred of the Hawkarmy but changed her mind and ordered, 'Let us divide them up and scatter them throughout our entire army. In this way they will strengthen all our forces and even train them. Soon all our forces could be likewise skilled and just as dexterous as the great Hawkarmy. Then there will be no jealousy against them.'

"This division and redistribution was carried out and the Hawks were so divided that they formed just five percent of each battalion."

And when Britania heard this story from Icedragon, who told her everything, she replied, "Icedragon, I am most pleased to know that our Hawkarmy was dispersed and broken up to appease the jealousy of a stupid queen. For now we will never need to fight them as a unit or as a fighting force, as one.

"Let troublemakers and destructive men be stood against and outlawed, even my uncle Summersailor. For we will win and overcome them."

Then Icedragon added, "I was able to speak quietly to some of our warriors and bring them here to join us, for there were some who would not change sides to join Warchariot. These were the Wavewarriors who feared Summersailor when he had challenged them to join or leave him. They had furtived into the background in the night. They came here in the armada which I brought, along with many deserters who seized the chance to take up swords against Snakeknife and Warchariot."

And Britania answered with a smile, ". . whom I almost destroyed with a short squall with my wings of storm. That was a gift I inherited from my godfather, the Truthteller of the Darts who lives high in the sky."

*****

CHAPTER ELEVEN
The Great Rout

After considering all the things that Icedragon had told them, Britania enquired further, "Tell us then, what is the state of Warchariot's army of Eagles compared to our Seagull Warriors?"

"They are stronger than we are," replied Icedragon, "now that our crack division serves among them. But I was never able to observe them, for I was watched by Winterwarrior who is the supreme fieldmarshal of the Eagles and next in rank under King Warchariot who distrusted me."

Then Britania nodded in agreement, "I understand. All four of us will sail and quietly infiltrate their outer flanks from all directions and assess their numbers, strengths and vulnerabilities."

So Whaleroarer, the Stormleaper and Icedragon all agreed.

Then Whitehair asked Britania if she could come with Streamflower, Maplewine and Willowflame. "Since it is only going to be for reconnaissance, we can help and we are all fully trained warriorwomen."

So the four heroes, each with their own warqueen and entourage all fully dressed in battle armor sailed out.

WarQueen Britania and her cousin Whitehair sailed to the east in the longboat named Truce.

Icedragon and Willowflame sailed north to the snow in the longboat, Nightbattle.

Stormleaper and Streamflower traveled south in the fast longboat known as Waterfight.

Whaleroarer and Maplewine came by the west, sailing out in the longboat called Winningspears, by the shortest route to reach the land of caves. They sailed by night to where Warchariot and his vile WarQueen

Snakeknife had camped out their army and pitched their tents in the centre of the peninsula.

Snowhills and trees and bushes of ice gave cover to the four groups of scouts as they scanned all that lay hidden among the trees before them.

The longboat Winningspear with Whaleroarer and Maplewine landed in a hidden cove on the west coast. Down to that cove there flowed a shallow river where the Eagles launched their boats to the open sea. Whaleroarer and Maplewine left the Winningspear in the hands of charioteers and able seamen.

Maplewine put on her accoutrements of war including a bundle of light javelins on her back and followed Whaleroarer along the banks of the snowy landingstream until at last they reached the hilly top and saw before them the Eagles' camp.

As they trekked, Whaleroarer uprooted many trees, stripped them by hand of all the little branches and threw them into the middle riverbed. He handled each tree like a javelin so that they landed and planted rootdown and upright along the middle of the launching stream and just below the surface of the icetop.

He explained to Maplewine, "These trees will grow into the muddy bed beneath the ice and snow. In the warm spring they will obstruct the passage of the Eagles' longboats as their warriors try to launch them. There will be no space on either side for boats."

Suddenly they had reached a ridge of trees and snowcovered bushes overlooking the Eagles' camp. All the grey tents and cool pavilions of the enemy stretched out across the field.

Gathered around one tent in a large circle were a dozen swordsmen performing tricks of swordplay. All had huge manes of golden hair and all were of the same breadth, shape and height. It was as though they all had been cast in the same mint. Their swords were hilted with pure ivory and each tall swordsman wore a bright red tunic.

Whaleroarer pointed to a warrior, "That is the royal guard," he whispered to Maplewine and then he pointed to a tent, "and no doubt that tent is the tent of

Warchariot and his vile WarQueen Snakeknife."

A great black cauldron brewed and bubbled there. Then out of the royal tent strode a young man, his skin as black as the brew in the black cauldron. With flaming eyes and huge powerful hands he held a three-pronged spear. When he plunged it into the boiling pot, flames shot up covering the entire spear.

"That is King Warchariot's general, the Ratrunner preparing his poisoned spear for cunning battle.

"And there moving within the tent is a huge warrior. That is King Warchariot. He is like a fierce mad bull and a sad implacable foe."

Maplewine tried to assess the warriors around the tents, "There are two armies but one of them is small and more highly skilled than the larger army. That small company must be the Hawks just brought into the field by Summersailor."

Then the scouts of the Eagles came back to camp and told the king and queen that they had seen enemies lurking in the hills above the camp.

So WarQueen Snakeknife took her makeup and her clothes of a warriorwoman and gave them to a servant girl who was elegant and looked like a warrior queen. The girl was told to walk around the camp.

When Maplewine saw the girl dressed as a warrior queen, she threw a light javelin at her before Whaleroarer had a chance to intervene. The javelin transfixed the singer and yet not one of the Eagles standing by seemed in the least concerned as she lay dying.

"It seems I have killed a harmless servant girl," said Maplewine. "I wish I had not been so thoughtless or so hotheaded. No doubt the dead one is no queen."

Whaleroarer tried to calm down Maplewine, "No matter for no one is harmless among the enemy for even a servant helps to build up courage in the foe."

Ratrunner had been told to note the place from where the javelin had been thrown. Then he threw out his fiery spear that shook out poisoned flames upon the Whaleroarer and on Maplewine, their charioteer and horses. However, the Seagulls' battle armor and shields protected them as they fled away to find a sheltered place.

Then King Warchariot sent three birds of message to tell his farout ranks that enemies were in the hills.

Maplewine threw more javelins that transfixed two birds in mid-air and they never took their message to the far battle flanks but the third bird escaped and soon delivered the warning. But rumor soon began to filter through the ranks that armies of Wavewarriors were invading.

It happened at this time that WarQueen Snakeknife had sent out for storytellers and songwriters, friendly to the Eagles, to come to speak and sing to boost the Eagles' bravery. When they came to the Eagles' camp, they were set upon and slaughtered in mistake by the Eagles who failed to recognize them as friends.

So Whaleroarer and Maplewine hid in the woods until it was safe to escape back to their boat.

At this time, Stormleaper and Streamflower came ashore in their boat Waterfight in the west coast of the peninsula when the Eagles were camped.

The moon rose on the camp of the Eagles that was now being stalked by a small company of Wavewarriors. The Mooncrow flew across the sky, reporting all it saw to the witches.

Warchariot sent out his magic killers led by a warrior blazing like a torch; a firefiend from the pit of endless flames, shaped like a human creature going to battle. As he loomed closer to the Seagull camp, waving his sword and yelling threats of firedeath, "I will burn to death all those whom I can touch," Streamflower yelled, "Aim at the snow-covered trees above him."

Then she and Stormleaper and their servants, all flung high their spears and javelins at the branches of the trees surrounding the man of fire. Surely and swiftly snow fell down upon him and all his flames were doused in the falls of winter. The man of fire burnt up and shriveled into a heap of ashes crumpling in the snow.

But hiding in the trees above the firefiend were three white forms of near-dead murderers. They had been waiting for a chance to kill the Seagull Warriors if they had escaped the fire. Now they fell from the trees. Pierced by the Seagulls' spears, they screamed for mercy.

"Yes, we will be merciful, for we will kill you," Streamflower answered coldly.

Stormleaper hacked them to pieces with his battle axe and cried, "I have no time to keep your heads. The wild dogs in the bushes roar and yelp."

Then Stormleaper seized a shovel and threw their pieces into the bushes where the wild dogs howled.

But other killers with glue holding together their barkwood suits were lurking in the fields and nearby forest.

The next morning at dawn Stormleaper asked his Wavewarriors if they could see any disguisers but they all shook their heads.

Then Streamflower peered into the woods ahead and warned the servants, "Beware of the wilddogs lurking ahead."

But Stormleaper shook his head in disagreement, "Beware nothing, those dogs did not eat us. Those are the dogs that ate our enemies."

Stormleaper lifted up two bits of meat leftover from the bodies of the disguisers and threw them far ahead into the tall trees that lined the way and also threw one out to the tall green grasses of the field. Soon the wilddogs had picked up the scents.

As Stormleaper and Streamflower and all their servants held up their slender javelins at the ready, the dogs smelt out the disguisers and threw themselves upon them and began to tear them apart.   Then Stormleaper and Streamflower let fly their thin darts and impaled the killers. The dogs dined on the bones then howled and lurked nearby, baying for more.

Slowly Stormleaper moved forward with Streamflower and their troop towards the camp of the Eagles.

Then Warchariot sent out his deadliest killers - the three Deathhead dwarfs. They were carrying the iron flails and swinging them with their powerful apely hands, all wrinkled and knarled. From each flail there hung seven strong chains with seven iron apples on each chain and sharpspiked poisoned thorns on every ball. The dwarf Deathheads, strutting from side to side like mad gorillas, rushed on the Seagull camp as Stormleaper's spears bounced briskly off their bodies. Even their eyelids were as hard as stone. Swinging their flails they walked a deadly walk, laughing and foaming at the thought of killing. Their heads, each with four eyes, rolled and roamed, looking out for prey.

One of the Deathhead dwarfs slipped for a moment upon the ice. Swift as a silver javelin, Stormleaper flung himself upon the ice and slid downhill to seize the Deathhead's flail then cut the fallen Deathhead dwarf to pieces. He threw himself, and his newfound Deathhead flail, in fury upon the other two Deathhead dwarfs and with his greater height and reach, he soon destroyed them both.

First the iron apple with venom thorns cut into the dwarfs' mouths. Their teeth and tongues were ripped out. The iron ball returned once more to smash the roof of the mouth. The white and bloody clot of brain was also ripped out with the apple, as blow on blow was flailed upon the dwarfs, by their own deadly weapon.

This ball cut them to mince so small that they might well have been passed through a cornmeal sieve. The Deathheads' flail sliced with sharp and frenzied butchery.

Even the wild dogs could not eat their bodies but pawed and picked the pieces of their bones that lay around like pebbles on the shore. In this way, all three dwarfs were smashed to pieces.

Then the Mooncrow once again spied over the camp of Stormleaper and told the tale to WarQueen Snakeknife.

"They are still alive. I just cannot believe it," cried Snakeknife, "send out our deadliest killers. Unleash the three friars from the pit of pestilence, led by the Abbot of Black Death. Those friars cannot be killed. They are dead already. Even their rats are dead, unnatural creatures from the deep abyss of pain where death is spawned. The three black monks have sick and ulcered skin. These are the twisted friars, concocting germs, breeding foul deadly strains of fever and cancer and inculcating all these into sick rats to set upon their foes."

So the undead friars were sent out to destroy.

Stormleaper saw these bent and twisted ghouls rushing close upon his troop. These ghouls were led by the Abbot of the Black

Monks. Stormleaper transfixed all four with his spears.

The monks began to struggle, squirm and squeal and bleed in anguish as they struggled to remove the rough spears from their bodies.

In their hot fever against Stormleaper, they released their rats, pointing them toward Stormleaper and Streamflower.

But the rats sensed that their masters now were weak and, though not dying, were bleeding in agony. So the rats seized their revenge upon the friars who had injected them with vile diseases and tortured them with cancers to pass on. The rats, creatures of death and deadly sickness, opened their mouths and tore the monks apart.

They set about devouring the devious Abbott whose strange vials and smoking test tubes had long woven webs of infectious pain and feverish death.

The rats and the monks of death suffered the pains their victims long had suffered before they all descended into the pit of pestilence from which they had been called.

***

Back in the castle of Warchariot and his WarQueen Snakeknife, the Mooncrow told them of how Abbot of Death and his monks and rats had all slipped back into the pit of pestilence in the ill universe.

Summersailor shook his head, "We may yet regret breaking up the great Hawkarmy, for these Wavewarriors have destroyed our main assassins and yet their WarQueen Britania has not acted and even Icedragon has not yet raised a hand. They have just bought time for their fragmented fleet to come together."

When WarQueen Britania landed her longboat in the east, she met with the Icedragon who was coming from the west of the bowlshaped peninsula of the Eagles.

At once the two agreed on their battle plans as they surveyed the peninsula from their chariots late in the night, watched over by the black Mooncrow.

As they made their plans, Britania pointed out, "The armies of the Eagles are too great for our Seagulls to attack them, head on head. Their fighting men would be too many for us now that we have lost our crack division with Summersailor and his skills of war. He is our kinsman and we much regret that he has left us. Perhaps he will come back and fight on our side once more, like you Icedragon. So let us quietly build up our fleet while we engage some of their heroes in single combat."

"Yes," Icedragon agreed, "That is the best plan, single combat. Soon the spring will come again and we need to give more time to Summersailor to think about his place with Warchariot. That is why we should not send out any boats or our main fleet until the spring has come and we can launch our farflung friends and ships."

Then the two great warriors sped their chariots forward and waved their swords at the Mooncrow in the sky. Icedragon shook his spear and called for combat as the black spy flapped her wings and screeched in hatred. Then the Mooncrow flew up high and drove the clouds away from the face of the moon and the light shone on a huge band of Eagles lying in wait, just ahead, where there was light enough to fight.

Then Icedragon challenged them, "I will accept you but only as one warrior at a time. I will fight against you all in single combat. Now is your chance to kill me, so seize your weapons."

Then Icedragon whipped his chariot upon them. It was a quick and effective onslaught. He steered his horses towards them, fiercely flinging his sharp and terrifying spears and javelins, hammered and molded from iron and tense steel, beaten with a strong arm in the fires of triumph.

A hero light glowed all around Icedragon, a halo of fire and brightness flashed about him as he called out his deadly oath of combat, "A battle is not a battle unless a hero has been death slaughtered or brought low in homage. I swear that I will slay great warriors or else I will myself be slaughtered here."

Then Icedragon took to slash and hack, and arms and legs and heads fell round about like the green boughs of pears and apples and plums, in the autumn of a red and yellow orchard, as the Eagles and their horses fled away.

Likewise, Britania gave out her battle challenge to the fleeing foe to bring them back to battle, "I do expect your bravest and your best. So let a high spirit and courage rise up in you, for what you do today will be long retold. Each one of you will be marked for what he does. The tale of each one's work this battleday will be recorded in the annals of war forever.

"Also, it will be remembered what you said, and how you boasted, in your nights of wine. So remember now your wineboasts and your pledges.

"Announce for me a single combat challenger. I will fight, one to one, with any warrior now or at any time that meets your courage. I will rise up, wherever you may stand, like a cock crowing suddenly in the cold dawn. I will flap my wings like a bird and go to combat with the heavy harness of battle across my shoulders."

But still the Eagles ran away and skulked behind the trees and bushes and rocks of the forest.

So Britania with warrior friends and Whitehair standing beside her took to the great longboat to scour the coastlands and flush out the foe. Her yellow skin glowed like the rising sun in its hazy mesh of red and blue. She was an oriental princess of power and speed and held the magic Bonespear in her hand. She steered her ship along the withering sea, hard cutting, throwing aside the waves like waste. The wind knifed keen into her face. It was like a charioteer spinning along an open road, with spears and swords and killer sythewheels slashing forward. So the boat flew, ringed around with swords and spears and in the prow of the boat stood Britania, like the rising sun.

A cold wind blew across those dangerous blades of weapons, set up and pointed by a gang of howling ghosts. Lean phantoms shimmered in a solemn imitation of servingmen all grinning and offering to serve up drinks. Long knives and daggers and sharp forks and spoons lay on the silver plates. Places were set by the bowing, scraping, obsequious spirit servants.

The specters invited all, My good lords, drink, they shimmered and grinned and beckoned, offering to deal the drinks of death to all the Eagles.

When the Eagle Warriors refused these invitations, Britania cried out to the Whaleroarer and to Icedragon and to

Stormleaper, "Let us go forward and wreck havoc among these Eagles."

Then Winterwarrior, veteran of many combats, stood with his warriors. A herolight shone all about him as he called to the men who followed him, "This story will be sung even among shepherds, wherever tales of war are told and retold."

Britania steered her boat ashore and her men set up her chariot and laid out the accoutrements of war. She had carved out paths of blood and bones so many times in the ranks of the enemy when she had trained with Shadowhero but now she was a skilled warrior.

Never did Britania slow nor even stop her speed but galloped over the Eagle's chariot leaving Winterwarrior wounded on the battlefield while the assassins lurking behind the wild Britania were left stunned and at a loss.

She kept control of her chariot as it flew over the chariot of Winterwarrior and pounded straight ahead into the battle. Britania rolled ahead and slashed and hacked. The ground shook over more than

1000 acres as she carved a path fit for a queen.

Spears of the deadly thousands of the Eagles erectly stood high up in the chariots, gleaming and fiercely glinting in the sunlight; a threat to all but those in the chariot. Across the seated legs of warriors there sat the swords waiting to be seized and wielded. Silver shields hung on elbows ready for use and helmets of burnished brasses crowned the heads.

Each horse was quick and easy to mount and steer with a strong bridle of twisted ropes and cords. In between the chariots roamed herds of extra horses, ready to be dragooned for the need of battle, steeds with large open nostrils and sharp eyes set in small heads. These steeds ran on broad hoofs and were easily caught and stopped. They were swift and dexterous for a sudden raid for when Britania flattened a road of red that was fiery and tempestuous and true as steel, she carnaged to take revenge for the killing of her father, Waterbear.

There was an aura of revengekill around her like the smell of a deadly wild boar when it strikes. When a hero even looked on this solemn soldier, the hero's heart grew weak and his arms tingled with dread.

The Eagles faces grew black with fear and some warriors lost their strength. Some even lost their minds just to approach Britania. Men, driven mad with fear, ran far away from her, screaming like ghosts. Some of the Eagles killed each other just to escape Britania's sword of battle and the gravedigger's inexorable destruction.

Her chariot advanced, leaving a wake of white and red dead bodies on the road just like the wake of foam behind her longboat.

As the ice began to melt, the small skiffs and the longboats of the Seagull Warriors edged out to sea, to invade the land of the Eagles.

Britania sailed her longboat over the waves, unshipped her weapons once again and drove her wild horses of war through the Eagle camp slaughtering many like a wild tornado.

As one Eagle lay dying, he cried out, "Let me die out at sea where I have lived among the seals and dolphins and the seaweed. Let me die with the smell of seasalt in my nostrils. Take me out there I beg of you, Britania."

Britania threw the bleeding man, in full view of the battle, across her shoulders, carried him to the sea and swam him out to where the Icedragon's boat lay near the shore. Then Britania swam back to join the battle.

So the Icedragon's men saw how Britania had brought the weak man out beside their boat and thought the dying man had been one of theirs who had been wounded in the battle ashore. The wounded man swam close to Icedragon's boat and asked the Seagulls to help him come aboard.

One of Icedragon's men stretched out his hand to pull the Eagle into the great boat but the Eagle, even as he was dying, seized hard upon the wrist of the Wavewarrior, pulled him into the sea with a sharp grip and drowned him with great force.

As the dying Eagle drowned the Wavewarrior, he cried out to all the Seagulls and the Eagles, "Death to all Wavewarriors. Even with my last faint gasp of breath I hold down a Wavewarrior and drown him."

And neither the Eagle nor the Seagull were ever seen again for the Eagle clung to the Seagull like the bite of a mad pitbull, through all their drowning struggles.

And all who stood ashore in the battle heard the boast of the dying Eagle as he drowned his foe. Many in the ranks of the Hawkarmy who were divided up among the Eagle's forces were watching. They saw what had happened and with what treachery and deceit the Seagull, their former friend and fellow Wavewarrior, had been murdered by the Eagle Warrior.

They noted this and stored it in their memories, but for now they mostly stayed in place for the sake of loyalty and also out of fear of Summersailor who was now fighting their former friends the Wavewarriors in the field of brutal and unforgiving battle. But some of the Hawkarmy secretly rebelled and mutinied against the Eagles.

*****

Chapter Twelve
Mistaken Identity

After this great rout of the enemy, Britania made evening camp for all her warriors in the remote forest, so that they could rest and eat and sleep.

Suddenly a woman in black rode past in a chariot drawn by deathly black horses. The chariot was of burnt cinderwood as though both woman and chariot had been through a fire. In her hands she held two black shields and two swords of glittering black. Her skin and eyes were darker than the night and three pupils moved around in both her eyes. She wore flowing robes of black silk.

The Shield of Roar cried out a call of warning that something dangerous had come into their camp.

Stopping her chariot in front of the Seagulls, the woman stared at Britania for a long time then drove away. She looked straight ahead as she disappeared into the shadows and the shades of the forest.

Then Whitehair told Britania, "Bad things will come for the look of that dark woman was long, deep and sorrowful. It frightens me. It is the harbinger of devildays ahead."

"That is War," Britania told her sadly, "We did not start it. Soon it will be finished."

Whitehair was still unsettled, "But I can see mindmadness and delusion ahead."

Britania answered thoughtfully, "Yes, I can see it too. I feel as though her eyes burned into my brain and stole a part of me, yet I remain whole and undivided."

Then Britania closed her eyes and bowed her head.

At that very moment, a sameshape of Britania appeared before her younger brother, Stormbolt, who was far away in his snowy training camp. The sameshape beckoned to young Stormbolt to join it in the chariot, a black and burnished chariot like that of the dark woman who had earlier stopped and stared at Britania.

A voice, like the voice of Britania, spoke to Stormbolt, "Your uncle Summersailor has gone over to the enemy so you must come with me now."

Stormbolt entered the chariot and it fled away into the snowy and the silvery fields.

Shadowhero ran outside and chased after the dark chariot, shouting, "Stormbolt beware. Was that really your sister or just an image of her counterpart from the pit?"

He paused and wept and shook his head, "But I am too old and cold to follow you. Perhaps one of our younger men should go to see if Stormbolt is being taken astray. I smell a pungent odor of burning embers."

Then he turned aside and shook in fear but others came to comfort him, "It was Britania. We all identified her. Even now you might hear her voice in the chariot. It was no sameshape mirage and no fetch."

Soon the two horses and the two ghostly forms in the chariot were silenced in the mists of swirling, flying snow. And so the sameshape of Britania had taken Stormbolt in the phantom chariot to the land of the Eagle Warriors.

King Warchariot with his WarQueen Snakeknife met with the four witches who conspired with their magic potions to suppress old memories in the mind of Stormbolt. So they gave him a new name, the warname of Strangelook and told him it was best for him not to know his true identity in the coming combats.

"You have not been here before, Strangelook, so you cannot know who is friend or foe but we will tell you."

Then Queen Snakeknife took King Warchariot aside and asked, "Why do we not just stab or poison him now that we have him in our power?"

But Warchariot replied, "No, I have other plans for his downfall. We can use his death to bolster the authority of our young hero Winterfire, the son of Winterwarrior.

"When Stormbolt is killed by one of our heroes it will be devastating to Britania and all the Seagulls when her younger brother is killed by one of our Eagle champions.

"Now that we have lost all our best assassins at the hands of the Seagulls, we need to have a great victory to bring together our uneasy factions."

Snakeknife replied, "I agree, Winterfire is indeed one of our heroes. A herolight shimmers all around his head and we do need him now that war is furious.

"Let us unleash the four sly witches of many spells and forms who can use many disguises to attack Stormbolt and defend Winterfire."

"Do so," replied Warchariot, "but remember to tell the four witches to remain down low and not to be seen much. Keep their cunning help a secret stab for victory or we will be blamed for ganging up on young Stormbolt and murdering him. We need to enjoy the glory of our victories."

But the evil WarQueen Snakeknife had her own plans for Winterfire, the son of fieldmarshal Winterwarrior.

Now, at this time, in the spellroom of the Mooncrow, young Stormbolt was being armed for combat. The servants helped set up his accoutrements with hardmail tunic and high boots of steel. They fitted a close helmet with a slat for eyesight over a woolen knitted face and head mask so that even his kinsmen would not know him.

The witches took a mist from the far sea, conjured up from the islands of the east and mixed it with herbs of forgetfulness. They gave it to Stormbolt to smell and drink so that his mind was not clear in its memories and they reminded him that his warname was Strangelook.

Suddenly the figure of an old man appeared at the barred castle window. He crept up to the window and croaked at Stormbolt, "Let me talk to you."

"Go away," cried the four witches, pointing their long fingers.

"What do you say, Youngman?" asked the old one.

"Please come in and welcome," replied Stormbolt.

The witches flung themselves on the door and locked it, screaming out curses on the old man's head as he disappeared at the barred window.

Then Landslink muttered in fear to the other witches, "It is the Truthteller. Keep him outside or our champion will see clearly."

But when the Truthteller stepped through the castle wall the four witches fled into the shadows screaming against him.

The Truthteller told Stormbolt who he was and that he had come to warn him. "Beware of false voices that misguide. You will fight one fight and then be celebrated forever and a day. . ."

Stormbolt replied, "If I could have only one day of glory and honor that is all that I would ever ask. I would be satisfied."

"That is well said," responded the Truthteller solemnly. "One great battle is all you will ever win. Promise me that your great combat will be all that you fight or all you seek to fight. Promise me that you will fight only one time."

Stormbolt promised, "I will fight only once."

The Truthteller bowed to Stormbolt in recognition of this solemn promise. Then he gave him a pebble on a string with a fishhook attached. "Take this fishhook and keep it by you on your battle belt. You will need it to defeat your many foes."

Stormbolt put the fishhook in his belt with care, "I am not going fishing but I thank you, Truthteller, for your help."

When he looked up again the old man had disappeared but Stormbolt's memory remained as confused as ever.

In the shadows of the castle, the four witches of kill - Windweasel, Rivershark, Meteoreyes and Landslink transformed themselves into wild animals ready to attack and to distract the two heroes as they battled in single combat with each other.

Windweasel took the form of a bald eagle; Rivershark took the form of a blood hungry shark; Meteoreyes took the shape of a maddog foaming and frothing at the teeth with deadly bite and Landslink took the form of a treesnake that hid and crawled with an envenomed spit.

Then the two warriors, Stormbolt and Winterfire were escorted forward, each with his henchmen, to the place of combat, a clearing in the woods near to the castle. Many of the warriors of the Eagles and the

Seagulls laid down their arms to watch the single combat.

The witches in their deadly animal forms were slinking and creeping along the branches, weeds and bushes as they hid in the riverbed of the forest.

King Warchariot and his sly WarQueen Snakeknife watched the combat from the battlements.

The witch Landslink, who was now in the form of a treesnake, raised her head out of her lair deep in the foliage. Stormbolt, throwing his chisel-pointed dagger, cut her head off. Then, with his swinging fishhook, he picked up the snakehead and threw it at the shark that jumped out of the water to devour him. The shark was choking on the venomed treesnake's bile as it fell back into the river coughing and choking.

The circling eagle swooped down upon young Stormbolt who swung his fishhook and ripped out its throat.

The half-dead eagle then flew at Winterfire and blinded him as bloody specks and feathers fluttered in his face, distracting him and turning him inadvertently from the fight. Winterfire beat away the specks of blood and all the dust of fluttering feathers from his mail helmet and his blurring eyes.

The maddog lurched at Stormbolt who stood back and seized an old hollow log that had been left by the Truthteller for Stormbolt's protection. Stormbolt rammed the log into the mouth of the maddog, who bit upon it strongly, sinking its teeth into the mossy wood so that the log stuck in the maddog's mouth. Then Stormbolt swung his fishhook with the pebble on the string into the hollow log with a great power so that it entered down the maddog's throat. The fishhook caught itself on the dog's heart and Stormbolt ripped it out with a sharp pull so that the dog rolled over and lay dead.

Then the four spirits of the witches flew back to the shades of their dark castle leaving the bodies of the savage killers: the shark, the tree-snake, the maddog and the eagle all lying dead before the young Stormbolt.

King Warchariot and his WarQueen Snakeknife stood up and yelled.

Warchariot cried out, "Either young Strangelook is very lucky or there is some kind of magic working on his side. In either case we need to dread this day."

And a deadly silence fell upon the watching hosts, for luck was on the side of Stormbolt. Swifter than the Eagle hero Winterfire, Stormbolt leapt high and flung his javelin straight through the throat and spine of Winterfire who staggered, slightly blinded by the dead eagle that the powers of win had tried to use to help him.

A mighty roar rang out in the forest glade as Winterfire seized the javelin that had transfixed his throat from front to back. He tried to pull the weapon out, then sighed and lay back in a pool of blood.

As Stormbolt cut off the head of the defeated Eagle hero Winterfire, the sly WarQueen Snakeknife seized the arm of Warchariot and with suppressed glee whispered, "What can we do now? We are well defeated. We have lost our hero, Winterfire."

"We have lost other heroes in the past," responded Warchariot, "We still survive."

WarQueen Snakeknife then cried out, "Perhaps this is not all bad. Strangelook is under our control and spells. Now we must hail him as our new leading champion. Most of our warriors will follow him and we will win the war against his sister Britania.

"Later, Britania must fight with her own brother and this can only work out well for us, for now Britania cannot win. No matter what the outcome may yet be, Britania loses. Even if she wins, she loses deep in her mind. For who could remain sane after she has slain her young brother."

Now that Stormbolt had killed their Eagle champion Winterfire, King Warchariot and his sly WarQueen Snakeknife changed their battlecries. They praised Stormbolt, now known as Strangelook, as their new champion.

So the two keen and eager armies threw themselves upon each other once more.

The Eagle army was urged by the four witches, the king and queen, to follow behind their champion Strangelook. They shouted for the armies to close ranks behind Strangelook their victorious hero and forcing him on to meet the Seagulls led by Britania.

Stormbolt, mindful of his promise to Truthteller not to fight a second combat, held himself back but cheers of victory and praises for his fighting swept the young Stormbolt forward to the foe. The force of his supporters mobbed and crowded the young champion forward in the battle to meet the young WarQueen Britania, in mortal combat.

As both armies flew upon each other, howlings of fear screeched out from the black spirit of the Mooncrow. The Shield of Roar cried out in agony foretelling of more destruction as Seagulls and Eagles were driven to frenzies of killing and maiming without mercy or conscience.

When Britania saw the mayhems and the savagery of the two armies, she asked, "Who is that fighting warrior leading the Eagles, killing all those before him like a scythe on the wheels of a chariot in the fire of battle?"

She was told, "That is Strangelook the new champion and hero of the Eagles."

Britania answered, "Is that so. Then I must kill Strangelook, their new champion, for only that can turn the tide of battle back in our favor now that we are outnumbered."

So she pointed her charioteer towards Stormbolt and swung her great axe high and balanced the Bonespear high upon her shoulder. It quivered and hummed for a hero's blood until Britania stood before her young brother Stormbolt.

But when he saw the weapons of WarQueen Britania, he recognized them. Stormbolt remembered them as weapons from a dream or sleeping vision, from where or when he did not know. But he knew that they were the weapons that would destroy him. He flung his spear at Britania but the throw was cold without a flash or flame.

The Bonespear needed only a brief flick from the fingers of Britania and it leapt to keep its foretold destiny and its thirst for hero blood, deep into the throat of Stormbolt.

Then Britania looked evenly at Strangelook and stabbed him through the heart with the broadsword and seized the Bonespear out of the neck and spine of Strangelook and took his axe and struck his head off.

As the head rolled away it moaned, "These are the weapons of my sister. So let me be remembered for the one fight that surely turned the tide of war."

Then Stormbolt died.

The many warriors who stood close by heard Strangelook's words and pondered them.

Britania did not understand but took the face mask and the helmet from the head of Strangelook who was really her young brother Stormbolt. When she saw what she had done she screamed aloud and wept.

And when the word went out that WarQueen Britania had been tricked into beheading her younger brother all the warriors standing nearby backed away and whether they were friend or enemy they all fled for their lives.

*****

CHAPTER THIRTEEN
Killfury

Britania set her mind to bury her young brother Stormbolt with honors in a longboat set on fire and sent to the Isles of Youth where all great warriors had gone before. But when she asked after the body of Stormbolt she was told it still lay cold upon the field of battle.

King Warchariot and his WarQueen Snakeknife had refused to honor him or even recognize him as one of their Eagle Warriors. Snakeknife had ordered the body to be left dead and dry, not to be desecrated but not to be venerated because the body had been visited with bad luck.

Britania was deliberate and dutiful, for deep anger and a great grief had come upon her when she had looked down upon the lifeless body of her young brother Stormbolt. She saw the brother who had been strong and skillful, loyal and honorable, become the victim of deceit and mind manipulation. His body was now lying grey and cut off like a broken branch.

Britania had been stunned when she killed Stormbolt and her mind was now struck frozen cold by the mask of death upon her brother's face.

As her personal servants carried the body of Stormbolt to the ship that was being prepared for the burning burial of a hero, Whitehair and the other ladies were silent and did not speak to Britania. For what words could be said that would make any sense or what tears could be shed that would bring any comfort on such a day?

As Britania watched the burial ship sail away into the distance, she spoke to all her fellow Wavewarriors.

"It is a shame upon me that there is left even one Eagle Warrior alive to tell the bitter tale of how, in anger and in haste, I killed my brother instead of the enemy. I wish that I had found an honorable death rather than this dishonorable victory.

Then a killfury rage came upon her and she poured herself out upon the Eagle Warriors and when the young WarQueen Britania killfuried she came suddenly in her nightwrath upon the camp of the Eagles. Those Eagle Warriors who were asleep were awakened by the sounds of war; the smashing of shields splitting as the axes ripped through them; shouting and screaming and the crumble of spears and javelins; breaking bones; the roar of fires; screaming women and children; the yelping and howling of the dogs and cats.

They strapped on their combat armor and rushed into the battle expecting to find an army attacking them. Instead they saw a lone warriorwoman in a killfury and one who fought like a thousand warriors.

The Eagles were confused and stabbed at each other and ran around in circles to defend against the long killfury of the young WarQueen Britania as she roared and slaughtered on for several days.

When all the Eagle army came out in force, Britania stood on a cliff and spoke to all their grim assembled warriors, "May Deathfate come to you who stand against me. Deathfate also to those who help you fight but I wish good days to those you leave behind. I challenge you to come fight Britania at any time of day or night you find me awake, or in my sleep, eating or resting, before my face or creeping up behind me."

So sly teams of killers were sent out by Warchariot and his wicked WarQueen Snakeknife to find and surround and slaughter Britania while she lay asleep. The killers were tense and quick-looking around, nervously jumping.

As they prodded and poked around in the forests at night they found a small fastsleeping camp in the shadowy darkness and fell upon it and slaughtered every soul. Then they fled away and came back in the daylight to see if Britania had been killed.

But once again the camp that they had murdered were only singers come from far off to tell tales of pastwars and sing the good oldsongs that had glorified the Eagles. All had been killed by the Eagles, in their terror of the young WarQueen's killfury. For the hard and rigid mask and trance of death, in the cold morning light, had settled on those who had come to sing and storytell to the Eagles. So many Eagle Warriors wept and moaned in sorrow.

Then Britania sent for all her Seagulls to rally in the cove of a high cliff and she addressed the warriors in this way, "Too many of our comrades and kinsmen have fallen because of the spells and delusions of our enemy.

"These Eagles cannot fight without attacks on our minds and thoughts and souls. Therefore, I urge you all to follow me now and I will go out and slay a hundred of them on each and every day. I ask you only to keep their other killers from throwing javelins at my back. Form yourselves into a high guard along that ridge and cut off their attempts to kill me from behind."

Splendid and glowing like a golden warrior, her yellow skin reflected the dawning light. A herolight shone all about Britania and a halo of fire and brightness flashed around her as she stood high upon the ridge and shouted to the assembled hosts of Eagles, "I say that neither flesh nor bone can flourish from your tired army, except what may escape from the mouths and claws of the ravens that attack you. Send me a hundred warriors every day to this wide sandy bay to fight with me and I will dispatch a hundred of your dogs each morning, for you are all unworthy of any single combat on my part."

Then a great shout of contempt and arrogance, a vast cry of derision, roared from the Eagles.

It was the longtime custom of the Eagles when they went into any battle for each man to lift up a granitestone and put it down nearby to form a mound. For each stone represented a warrior gone into the battle. When they returned from their hardfighting, each warrior carried away his own lifestone and the stones that remained were counted and totaled up. The stones that were left behind were the tally of the number of warriors who had been slain in combat, who never would return to carry away their lifestones from the mound memorial. In this way, the remaining stones gave a quick number of those who had died in battle.

At the screech of dawn they sent out a hundred men and chariots to meet Britania. And as the rooster crowed, Britania met them and poured out upon the hundred men like the molten burning copper from a furnace flowing into the cast of a weaponmonger. Britania slaughtered them in a torrent of red sword.

So Britania called out to the one hundred, "Do not trouble to make a cairn for I will make one for you."

Then Britania made three separate mounds and piled them high along the ridge that overlooked the bay. One mound was made of weapons from the dead. One mound was made of bodies that had died. The third cairn was built up of severed heads of the grinning hundred who had been beheaded.

The young WarQueen Britania now tiring from her killfury returned to her own ships. And the hero, now as hot as molten copper, was plunged into a cold vat of icewater. She remained hot and breathing hard but she was plunged again into a pool of cool sea water to calm down her head. Soon the cool water sizzled like a hot geyser. For a third time Britania was plunged into a cold cauldron of brine and seaweeds. Only then did the water bubble to a mild warm.

Then a mindmadness came upon her as she shivered and trembled but found no place to hide.

She gave her Bonespear back to the Icedragon along with the crown of brave Waterbear, her father.

The sharp-eared Shield of Roar that shouted warnings, she gave to her other heroes but she retained the Rainbowsword that sent a rainbow high into the sky.

Britania tried to escape into the clouds or drown deep in the sea. Then she fled to the great waterfall to join the voices, ghostily and madly swirling in the fountain.

Yet she could find no place where she could fly to; no perch upon the clifftops of the caves. And the Wavewarriors raised a great howl to help her, a huge shout of support for their great hero but she did not hear them shout because the spirits of the waterfall screamed louder and louder. Britania fought hardsword against the waterfall. As she warred with water demons and delusions, her sword flashed many colors of the rainbow. But deeper voices from the wells of demons called on Britania to join eternal voices and stay with them forever in the pools.

As the echoes from waterfiends spoke to Britania, she fought with the demons of the waterfalls as their voices made strange words. "No more the time for war. Why should you slash and cut off heads and limbs? Why should you killfury and destroy yourself? Isn't the sea around us still and isn't the earth under our feet, the sky overhead? What has changed in the world around us as a reward for all the cruel mayhem? The harvest of the combat is dead bones."

So there she stayed locked in a dreamworld of guilt and persecutions in her tormented mind.

*****

CHAPTER FOURTEEN
The Old Bathhouse

Then the sly WarQueen Snakeknife congratulated King Warchariot that many hundreds and thousands of heroes and warriors were pouring back to the Eagle camp now that Britania had run away, leaving the Wavewarriors without a leader.

Warchariot gloated and washed his hands with air as he watched the moving mass of men and metal weapons as the Eagle Warriors returned home once again.

As more ships of the Eagles sailed into the harbor, they set their linen sails and built their blue awnings to protect them from the high sun and the spray. Then they wined and dined as they listened to their pipers and harpists and their storytellers celebrate the deeds of war and conquest that would follow when they pursued the fleeing Seagulls.

So the Eagles set up their revenge camp nearby and arose early the next dawn and put on their coats of brightest mail, shining beneath helmets of gems and gold and all their finest weapons for war. They strutted like cocks crowing in the cold dawn for the Eagle Warriors were coming back to strike against the Wavewarriors now that their WarQueen Britania had gone to battle with the demons of the waterfall.

While Britania fought with the ghosts of the waterfall, the Eagles never once dared to follow her in case she turned away from slaying spirits. But the Truthteller had gone to the great waterfall to find her.

The demons of the waterfall told Britania to lie down and die because she was mad. They tried to persuade her to take her own life.

But when the Truthteller found her he commanded the demons, "Be quiet. Tell no more lies, demons of the waterfall, for I am the Truthteller and my word is power. Your lies can only lead to self-destruction. You can survive only for a little while. Even now you and the waters must fall silent."

Then he turned and spoke to Britania, "Come Britania, let us go back to your own Seagulls. Even now they are in great danger and need you."

So after some words of direction from the Truthteller, Britania entered her chariot and made her way back to rejoin Icedragon and Stormleaper and the rest of the Wavewarriors.

Meanwhile, the Eagle Warriors were encouraged by rumors of Britania's madness and threw themselves on the ranks of the Wavewarriors and tried to split the Seagulls into two parts.

WarQueen Snakeknife ordered the Eagles, "Split up the foe and cut off the vanguard with their two great heroes, Icedragon and Stormleaper and their entourage. Drive them along the paths to the Old Bathhouse.

"I have made some improvements there, especially to help new visitors to take the waters. Those old steam spas are good for the spine and energy."

Warchariot laughed as he washed his hands in invisible water.

As Stormleaper and Icedragon whipped their chariots towards the coast, they saw the bathhouse.

Britania pointed towards the iron house, "We could make a stand there with all our camp."

When they arrived they found that there was fire and water there. The walls were made of iron. It would have been a great place to defend if they had been attacked.

They saw that the windows were well barred for use by archers and yet it did not seem to be heavily defended.

As the dozen Seagull chariots drove up, the four or five defending Eagles ran off.

The two grim heroes, Stormleaper and the Icedragon, dismounted, drew their swords and entered. The house was filled with empty cubicles for changing and holding clothes. Ranged all around were covered steambaths and beside them were chairs, tables and mirrors.

An old woman in her nineties sat in one corner before a mirror. Two young servant girls attended her with combs and files and scissors and paint and makeup brushes. The room had some tables with fine fruits, candles and flowers.

The ancient lady pointed her finger at the heroes, "Do not dare to enter here. For this bathhouse is reserved for me, just now."

Stormleaper bowed low and then asked, "Who are you?"

"I am Queen Rainbow, mother of the Queen."

"You are the mother of the Eagle WarQueen Snakeknife?" he exclaimed.

"I have told you so. Get out or I will call her."

Then Stormleaper and Icedragon bowed and removed their helmets and walked backwards to the door.

Outside the bathhouse they spoke to WarQueen Britania and their two warrior queens, Streamflower and red Willowflame, "It seems we have a hostage. She is the ancient mother of Queen Snakeknife. But she does not realize who we are."

Britania spoke to Streamflower and Willowflame, "Go inside and bind her but please be careful not to hurt her and do not let her escape."

Suddenly the two young servant girls, who had been helping Queen Rainbow, came out with tubs of dirty water which they threw down the drain.

As Britania, Stormleaper and Icedragon entered the bathhouse, the servant girls walked away. A short scream rang out as the old lady was seized and gagged and bound.

A few minutes later, some of their lookouts who had walked around the bathhouse reported to Icedragon and Stormleaper what they had seen, "We have checked the bathhouse. Down in the basement smiths are stoking and filling the furnaces with coal and logs and branches. Their furnaces heat the water in the tanks below the baths. Steam rises through small holes into the air beneath the copper baths. The baths are honeycombed with holes for the hot steam to enter. Each bath is covered with a leather cape that keeps the steam in the bath. Servants control the flow of the hotair by pushing leather trays, backward and forward, underneath the baths. In the hot basement, the smiths are shoveling fiercely and fanatically as though expecting some clients of importance for the baths."

Then Icedragon thanked the guards and answered them, "That may be so, for Queen Rainbow is here. Perhaps there are others of her house expected. Let us go inside and close the great iron door."

Inside the iron house, when the door was closed, the Seagulls settled down to eat and sleep. After a little while, Britania sat up and saw small bubbles crackling at the drains as it grew hot and hazy. She was puzzled and uneasy at this sight and soon began to think of strange events.

In curiosity, Britania pulled off the gag plaster from the frail queen's mouth and asked the old lady, "Why did your servant girls never come back to help you after they had carried out two little tubs of dirty water?"

Queen Rainbow replied, "The dirty water flowed from the high steps down to the lower floor. It seems the drains recently became blocked."

Then Britania cried aloud, "Why did this Queen's small guard all run away? Waken up all. We are caught in a trap. The drains are blocked. The doors and windows likely are now locked!"

Stormleaper awoke and, startled by Britania's alarm, pulled back the curtains from the metal window, "Iron shutters." He cried, "What fools we are. The shutters and doors have been recast in iron and fitted tight. We are sealed."

Icedragon kicked and tore at the front door but only the wooden cladding came away and under the wooden surface was solid iron.

Then Icedragon cried aloud, "We are locked up and sealed inside an iron box, an oven that is slowly being heated and stoked up by six strong smiths and furnacers below."

Britania and Willowflame were now distraught. Streamflower began to weep and scream and beat on the iron walls. They jumped upon the tables as the bubbling water crept higher on the floor.

Queen Rainbow laughed. "My daughter is WarQueen Snakeknife. When she finds that I am here in person she will order us released. Then you must fight to stay alive or she will surely kill you. She is a warrior Queen of many weapons."

Then Icedragon shook his head, "If Warchariot or Snakeknife had wanted a fair fight they could have had one and without all this deception and these contraptions."

"What do you mean? My own dear daughter, Snakeknife, would never let me die by your crude hands."

"You are not threatened by our hands," said Britania, "but by your treacherous daughter's hands. You need to know that you are not a hostage as we once thought. No, Queen Rainbow, you are a sacrifice and bait set for us to entrap us so that we can all be boiled or roasted alive."

"You are a liar. If I am not a hostage then set me free."

"Do so now," Britania nodded towards Icedragon.

As they released Queen Rainbow she knocked her makeup box down the stone steps, where it rolled over and over.

Queen Rainbow ran to the great door and banged upon it, crying, "Snakeknife my daughter, this is your mother. Set me free."

Not a sound or answer echoed through the door which stood as immobile as a sheer cliff.

Queen Rainbow beat with her fists on the door and shouted, "Tell me, my daughter if you can hear me?"

As a clear voice on the outside of the door rang out, the fingers of Icedragon tightened in anticipation on the Bonespear but the door remained as solid as a rock.

The voice of WarQueen Snakeknife echoed through the iron door, "Be quiet mother or you will embarrass me before my warriors. They will think me ruthless. You cannot have long to live in any case and it is nice to die saving your daughter and my dear king and all our loyal men from the crude butchery of these Wavewarriors. Just think of me as being a heart attack."

Queen Rainbow wept and pounded on the door until at last she realized that she had been set up as bait to catch the Seagulls by her own daughter Queen Snakeknife.

Streamflower took pity on the old lady and put her arms around her.

Then Willowflame said, "Come with us. Sit down beside your table on these steps for we will never harm you."

But the old Queen Rainbow was sick and trembling and, a second time, she dropped her dressing box upon the floor. It rolled over and over, through the hot and steaming bubbles that were building up, as the watery temperature rose higher.

"Look there," said Britania, "See that tumbling box and watch how it rolls over and over again. This old iron bathhouse also is a box. We are caught in a boxtrap. Why can we not make this big box roll over?"

"Just so," replied the Stormleaper, "If we could only roll this box down to the shoreline we could avoid the fires burning below us. Already this iron box is getting hotter.

"The steam is in the air, sweat on our brows. Hot water pours from small pipes into the tanks below the copper steam baths.

"If we can overturn this iron bathhouse with a great push the shock of being battered against the sides will cause us bruising, even some injury. So let us try this but with some precautions.

"Those cubicles of steel are strong and fixed to the walls and ceiling. Let Britania and her two ladies put their arms around Queen Rainbow and lock themselves inside a cubicle with the old one between them. This will buffer most of the shock of crashing this great bathhouse over the rocks that lead down to the sea.

"Also, pull out the small soft waterpipes where they pump the water into our tanks in case those small pipes might impede our effort to break away from the hot furnaces. Once we have overturned this bathhouse we know that they can roast but never boil us. I thank the powers of good for this small mercy."

The ladies locked themselves in the cubicle and the men hacked and broke off the small pipes where hot water trickled into the steam tanks. Some others tied down the furniture at the wall where they would throw themselves so as to add a little extra weight to their joint effort. Hot water poured out from the broken pipes and hissed and bubbled on the heated floor.

Then the heroes and charioteers threw themselves hard against the wall with the piled-up furniture. The third time that they threw themselves against it, the wall buckled and bent under the weight of their combined assault. The bathhouse trembled, poised on its edge, then shook and tumbled over then the house fell flat on its wall side.

The enemy outside the bathhouse could see underneath there was revealed the open burning furnace with flames shooting high into the air. The smiths piled on and shoveled coal and wood, toiling like slaves to heat the old iron bathhouse. And so intent were they, they did not stop even when the bathhouse rolled over on its side.

When WarQueen Snakeknife saw the flames from the furnaces leap high and send up clouds of billowy smoke she cried out loudly, "Stop it you fools. Save your fuel. Can you not see that you are heating the air?"

The men stood back, relieved and wiped their brows as the bathhouse crashed again and again as it rolled over and came to rest down on the rocky shore.

Warchariot strode upon the hillock crest and placed his arms akimbo and looked down. He ordered the master smith to kneel before him and drew his sword and asked, "Will your work stand?"

The master smith looked down, "No sign of life. The bathhouse may be moved but will never break. Nothing on earth will open it, my lord."

Warchariot and his sly WarQueen Snakeknife laughed loud and long.

"Well," said Warchariot to the master smith, "Don't stand around and waste your time. Take all your men and move the faggots and tinderwood and pile the coal and logs against the old bathhouse. Set it afire. Perhaps it will take longer to roast that crew alive, rather than boil them. Even if the sea comes in to douse the fires, then slow starvation is the fate of many in this poor world, so why should they escape it? Or what if they should drown under the sea? The might of the Seagulls still would be abated."

Then storytellers and singers came to report to Warchariot and Snakeknife on the other body of Seagulls who had been cut off from the group now trapped within the old bathhouse.

"They are weak and vacillating without a leader. And even as we speak those free Seagulls are being scattered abroad and cut to pieces."

Warchariot laughed again to hear this news and Snakeknife washed her hands with air and sneered, "Cut them or roast them, bury them alive just like the ones now trapped in the old bathhouse. Drown them, what is the difference?

"Come let us call on these songwriters to celebrate our victory. Let us eat and drink and sing the songs and listen to the tales of how we triumphed."

Inside the bathhouse the Seagulls crawled and creaked and stumbled from the crash but no one seemed to suffer but Queen Rainbow, who held her heart and gasped.

They all lit candles and searched the iron walls for cracks or breaks but found none.

"This is a fortress and a coffin," said the Icedragon. "I can hear outside the sound of digging. Soon we will be buried."

Then Queen Rainbow called the ladies to her side and whispered, "Goodbye. You have tried to save my life but I am old and cannot long survive this turmoil."

She took a chain and locket from her neck and gave it to Streamflower, "This is for all the ladies and warriors in this deadly cabin, for you were all entrapped here by my daughter. Here in this locket is the cameo of one I loved, long, many long years ago. Alas I left him, only to marry a king. Later my daughter was born, the offspring of a king and his bad blood. That daughter now is known as Snakeknife, the WarQueen of the Eagles.

"So take this locket. Open it when I die. Maybe this man in the locket picture may still remember me. I am too weak to call upon him now but he is the one who has the power to save you."

When Streamflower took the small locket from Queen Rainbow she kissed the old one gently on the cheek. Then the old lady seemed to become young again and died.

Streamflower was distraught as she opened the little locket. Inside she found a picture of a young Truthteller, whom she did not know.   As she wept in anger and frustration that the old lady had been speaking in riddles, she threw the locket against the iron door of the trap.

Suddenly a bright light flashed and filled the room and the door of the iron bathhouse flew wide open and Truthteller stood before them, tall and erect. He spoke not one word but stepped forward, took Queen Rainbow in his arms and walked outside.   Then he and the dead Queen disappeared into thin air as she was carried far, far away to the Islands of the Young.

The Eagle Warriors lurking outside, hoping to kill any of the Seagulls who escaped were blinded by the bright appearance of the Truthteller. They covered over their eyes and ran away.

Then Britania cried out, "See there. The Eagles have fled from the celestial darts of the Truthteller. Put on your armor and your shields of war so that when we burst out we will surely bring terror like a river bursting through its banks."

When they rushed outside they were indeed an ocean. They were flowing like a molten fire, a fierce fountain from a rock pouring down upon the plains. As the Seagull Warriors flew out of the boilerhouse in their full armor of war they were like birds flying from a falconer's cage.

Then the young WarQueen Britania along with her warriorqueens Streamflower and Willowflame and her heroes, Icedragon and Stormleaper flew down and changed into their human selves again as they flapped their wings and settled on the deck of their boat.

Leaving their magic forms as birds of prey, they took their places in their boat of war and sailed back to the Wavewarrior castle to rejoin the rest of the Wavewarriors.

*****

Chapter Fifteen
New Beginnings

Meanwhile, at the castle of the Eagles, Warchariot and his WarQueen Snakeknife talked about their recent encounters with Britania, WarQueen of the Seagulls. They were angry and determined to bring about the final downfall of the Wavewarriors. So they consulted once again with the witches Windweasel, Rivershark, Landslink and Meteoreyes.

"We will wait till we feel that the time is right and then lure the Wavewarriors to this castle for talks of peace with their enemies, the Eagles," said Landslink, "A castle of supposed peace but a place where words of war will prevail to bring confusion among the Wavewarriors."

As the four witches began to work their magic, Windweasel clutched and then unclutched the air with her sharp wrinkled claws and sneered with her toothless mouth, "Let us send out our many-colored message birds to lure the Wavewarriors to the castle. We will unleash the hounds of wicked words and set them on the Wavewarriors who will be torn apart like lambs by foxes; for there is nothing as dangerous as dangerous words."

Rivershark agreed with warted lips and sniggered as she wiped away her dribble, "Then let each man give his word of honor not to attack each other and to lay no hand or weapon upon each other until they leave the walls of the castle."

Then Meteoreyes, whose eyes were burning flames, cried out, "Let us call up a spellmist all around so that no one will know us as we are for if they did they would not trust us."

"Agreed," Windweasel croaked and hid her face. "Let us be seen as great beauty and smell like the lavender of summer days and have soft voices of whispering nymphs."

Landslink agreed with all these boastful words of snare, "We will have food and wine to lure them in and once inside we will control the warwords."

When the time was right the witches let fly out the birds of message that changed into the form of singing damsels. They sang out invitations to the castle inviting both the Wavewarriors and Eagles to come to eat and drink and listen to the hospitality of the queens of peace as the four vile witches had falsely called themselves.

When the servile invitations had gone out to the sweet music of the moon to come and relax and listen to tales of wars long gone by, the Wavewarriors replied, "Yes, we will come if our own songwriters and musicians and our singers also come with us to tell our versions of the tales of war."

Then the messengers transformed into gulls once more and flew back to the castle where a sumptuous meal was prepared for every champion and fit for the nobles of both the Wavewarriors and the Eagles.

The four witches went up to the parapet and looked across the plains. There in the distance they saw four chariots coming and behind those chariots clouds of dust as of many men and horses.

Windweasel shaded her eyes from the sun as she watched the approaching chariots of the Wavewarriors. Then she called for a servant girl, "Come here young woman, your eyes are fresh, look over the plain and tell us whatever you can see in greatest detail."

The servant girl called out, "I see the first of four great chariots, gleaming of gold and silver in the sun. It is drawn by two huge seahorses galloping in time together.

"Inside the chariot are four ladies of beauty and, sitting on their knees, three gangling birds with lean and bony legs and flapping wings. The birds' necks are bent and long and thin. Each bird has a large and drooping bill that speaks out words."

Rivershark spoke to the others, "Those are the three message cranes of the WarQueen Britania that scan and search the skies for a forewarning."

Then she asked the young clear-sighted girl, "Tell me. Are there any men in the chariot?"

The girl replied, "No, only fine ladies of great breeding and beauty all dressed like warriorwomen of the Seagulls."

Landslink thought for a moment and then addressed the others, "Those ladies must be the young WarQueen Britania with her three ladies-in-waiting.

"She enjoys the trust of her three birds. For even now she throws them high in the air and each one flies around the other chariots. There, one cries, 'Do not come, no, do not come' while another screeches out, 'Go past the castle.' Again, 'Go past the castle' and the third crane screams at the third following chariot, 'Get away.' Again it screams out, 'Danger, get away' but still the chariots continue to come."

"Ah, good," cried Meteoreyes, as the witches chortled, "they are coming towards us despite all the warnings and we must welcome them with open arms."

"The first chariot stops on the plain and does not approach perhaps it waits for other chariots to join it."

Then Rivershark cried out, "What is that roar, that muttering turbulence, that growling echo?"

The servant girl continued to tell what she saw, "I see a great company of fighting men in chariots with weapons gleaming in the sun coming in the distance. It must the Wavewarriors."

Upon arrival the ladies were greeted by servantgirls and shown to their private quarters in the castle.

Later in the day, the four witches in their disguise of beauty welcomed the fieldmarshals of the Wavewarriors as they all wined and dined. They presented each champion - Icedragon, Whaleroarer and Stormleaper - with a golden cup of wartriumph that claimed each hero was the conqueror of them all to sow the seeds of jealousy among them.

Landslink muttered to the other witches, "Remember, show no surprise or anger as they breathe in the airs of our enchantment. The men will see us as they wish to see us."

"Isn't it always so?" murmured the Rivershark, "but let us arrange these things as best we can. Send out now for the coming of the Eagles for their presence will unnerve and surprise the Seagulls. Soon we will have the Seagulls broken up for they are not expecting to meet Eagle Warriors. But warn Warchariot and Queen Snakeknife to keep into the background for they might well be the target of revenge for they murdered Waterbear, the father of Britania.

"But Flyingbat and Cragfox and our other Eagle heroes such as Oakhill, Winterwarrior (who is still recovering from his encounter in a recent battle) or Ratrunner may well engage some of the Wavewarriors in fighting talk. So they could help to lay the foundations of bad feelings and resentments for the days ahead. The bloodiest of bloody wars begins with words."

When Britania and her ladies entered the hall, they looked around in amazement to see the heroes of the Wavewarriors consorting with the hostesses.

And Britania shouted at her three fieldmarshals, "Think of your foot soldiers and see that they get food while you sojourn here wining and dining. I have come here to protect you with my cousin, Whitehair and my ladies-in-waiting, Willowflame and Streamflower and Maplewine. They are all armed and trained as warriorwomen with swords and shields and helmets, javelins and dirks to act as witnesses in any disputes.

"I tell you there are stirrings and rumors of preparations for war and these grim gatherings of many forces is all because my father, King Waterbear was murdered by lies and in treachery."

As Britania left the gathering to attend to her warriors outside the castle, her three fieldmarshals cried out, "Leave us to rest for a while. These lovely hostesses are most kind and attentive."

And the Wavewarriors laughed and sang and drank and held up their fine golden cups of champions.

The next morning in the feasting hall the Seagulls and the Eagles sat around eating and drinking.

The witch Windweasel reminded those present, "Remember all the men can collect their weapons and shields only when they leave and that you are under oath to use no violence against any man while you are in this castle. Whoever breaks his word will be put to death by all the others for we have all agreed between us to have a time of peace."

Suddenly a treacherous Eagle Warrior known as Ratrunner spoke to the Icedragon, "Your poor performance in battle is well known. I speak to you as a friend. What do you say?"

"Well," replied the Icedragon, "I must admit that my horses and my horsemanship are clumsy at times. It is well known how ponderously my chariot turns around in combat and how each chariot wheel digs a deep ditch that lies open for a year. Slowly but surely is my combat motto."

Icedragon then smiled and nodded to Ratrunner.

Ratrunner bowed and laughed, "I told you so. You are the slowest of the slow in battle and one day your clumsiness must result in death."

"Well, I cannot agree," said the Icedragon, "I have never yet been the loser in a combat and horsemanship is not the only story.

"Like a cock crowing suddenly in the cold dawn, to rise up like a bird and go to combat with the heavy harness of battle across my shoulders, I have been strong to gallop over fords and kick up a great spray against the enemy, flying into the faces of the foe in singlehanded combat, skill and fury. I have breasted rains of flying javelins with only one great shield and a handful of spears. Nor can any hero meet me in single combat. I have looked down upon the bones of many and I will still practice my chariot feats in days to come before both kings and heroes."

"Oh, really so? I will believe your boasting only when I can see it with my own eyes." Ratrunner sneered.

Icedragon laughed in scorn. "This is a strange meeting for friendships. Yes, here there is a low breeze, an underflow of jealousy and resentment and near-hatred that lurks beneath the surface of casual manners. What kind of company is this? Your own weak fantasy is far from reality."

"You are a strange one to talk of fantasy with all your boasting, bragging and arrogant bluster," said Ratrunner as he sneered at the Icedragon.

Icedragon replied, "I am content to wait until one day I meet you on a field of single combat."

Then the Icedragon moved away to talk to friends.

Landslink opened a small box that she had taken from the servant of Whaleroarer and cried out, "A dead dog! Who has dared to bring this here - a dead dog into a house of feasting? Remove this vermin rubbish from our banquet."

Then Whaleroarer stepped over to his charioteer Strongherd, "This is my dog Guardhunt! How can he be dead so soon? I left him tethered, fed and content."

"Master, Guardhunt went missing and I ran hither and thither, up and down and everywhere. I called for him, whistled and looked high and low.

"I met Cragfox and he told me, 'You'll find your dog dead on the shore,' and sure enough he lay there, all limp and wet and lifeless, drowned I think, by the hand of Cragfox, the cold killer of dogs."

"There is no need to speculate," said a voice from among the crowd of Eagle Warriors, "for here I am, Cragfox. I drowned the dog."

"Why did you murder him?" asked Whaleroarer."

"I did not murder it. I merely drowned it."

"And yet, you tied a stone around his neck and threw him in the sea. The tide returned and my drowned dog was thrown in on the tide?"

"Well, yes. I hope that that was not too hard on you. After all, a dog is only a mutt to us and we can find plenty more for next to nothing. So, no harm done, I believe you will agree."

Then the four witches rubbed their hands gleefully to see the Whaleroarer look so miserable. For he looked like one who wore shackles of sorrow and handcuffs of misery; to be led down a path that leads to death.

Whaleroarer took the small coffin with the dead dog. "My good old dog is dead. In the day of battle combat he stood by me. He was my friend and guard and true defender, in chariot, in duel and in the field. My good old dog - what a cold, lonely death, to die at sea."

Cragfox replied in regret to the Whaleroarer, "I was misled by one of our hostesses. The one with eyes of burning flame told me she had come by a report that a bad black and white shepherd dog was running rabid and terrifying the horses where they were on rein and could not escape. She asked me go and chase the dog out to sea.

"I know the shoreline well for I have often patrolled and mounted a guard upon that region to keep a lookout for our enemies. I did not know the dog meant so much to you. Do please remember all this is about an animal. This whole event is a misunderstanding and outside the bond and promise of our agreement not to engage each other in deadly combat. You cannot break your oath over the death of a dog."

"I know it, I have no intention of it," said the Whaleroarer as he sipped his wine.

Cragfox, lean, dark and watchful then walked out into the thin chills of the murderous night.

Whaleroarer muttered out a curse, "May he who caused my poor dog to be drowned, one day be drowned in the dread sea."

Then Flyingbat, one of a family who hired out to kill for gold and silver, remarked to Stormleaper, "Cragfox, now that he has said he is sorry for the dog's death, takes the whole matter as over and done with but he is very anxious to leave nevertheless for he besneaks himself out into the dark where he is at home. Few will be able to overcome him there and all because he killed a dirty dog and the dog's owner moans.

"Stormleaper, I can tell you truly and for certain who killed your father when you were a child. That is, you must agree, much more important that any killing of a mangy whelp. Wouldn't you like to know who killed your father? I heard it happened in your father's bedroom inside your fastness, windows and doors full locked."

And Stormleaper started up, "Yes, I well remember. It was a mystery. I thought it supernatural because my father was found murdered inside his locked bedroom."

Then Flyingbat slyly told his tale to the Stormleaper, "Oakhill my elder brother often boasts about the night he killed your father. Perhaps that is the reason why he has not come here. He is too kind to cause offense.

"Oakhill tells of how he dressed in a black suit and mask and crept into your fortress in the dark hours when all your family were feasting. He crept into the rafters above the bed in the steel room where your father normally slept. The windows and the barred door had been locked but the skillful burglar Oakhill unlocked them. Silent and motionless he hid there clinging to the rafters and beams until, long after dark, your father came to sleep.

"Then looking down upon your father, Oakhill stretched down his spear and held it till the dawn light filtered into the room. The weapon pointed at and almost touched your father's heart. Then he leaned on the spear and fell down hard upon it piercing the heart and tearing it apart without a single scream from your sleeping father."

The stunned Stormleaper took note of every word as Flyingbat continued with his tale.

"Oakhill seized up the keys lying beside the bed and let himself out. And once outside the bars of the bedroom door he locked the door again and threw the ring of keys under the door to fall beside the bed. Down the stairs he stole with a black-tarred sword and shield in his blackened hand and let himself out through a small cellar window.

"Later your family found your father dead inside his locked room. Some people thought that magic had been worked. My brother Oakhill gained a fortune for this deed, paid to him by your father's enemies – Snakeknife and Warchariot.

"Now we are wealthy we would do the same for you and likewise kill your family's foes or rivals for a good price. It is our business and I have nothing against you. It's all just money."

"Thank you," replied Stormleaper the Wavewarrior. "Let me just think about it for a while."

Flyingbat continued, "We would do a good job for you, if we were well paid.

"You can see that Oakhill is a cunning warrior. No one has ever been known to stand against him. He has disposed of many who were thought to be invulnerable."

"Of course and I will think it over," agreed Stormleaper.

Then Stormleaper moved away and joined the company of the Eagle fieldmarshal Winterwarrior and his deputy Summersailor who were trying to be peacemakers in the gathering. And Winterwarrior whispered quietly, "Those words were spoken only to provoke. See that you lay no hand or weapon on him. Flyingbat is a boaster. Do not break our agreement. Do not force us ever to behead you for the sake of honor for I have great respect for the Wavewarriors."

"Please believe me Winterwarrior I will not break our bond. I am attached to this poor head and I will not desert it for it is too bowed and broken to be abandoned."

"Good man, Stormleaper" said his old friend Summersailor as he gripped hard upon the upper arm of the Stormleaper.

Then Stormleaper left the food and wine to walk outside into the quiet of the night. He took his leave from the gathering with a low bow, a sad respect but with a need to go outside and ponder the events.

Outside the hall of wining and dining he met with the WarQueen Britania who was talking to some of the Hawkarmy Warriors.

When she asked about the goings on inside he told her all that Flyingbat had said to him.

"And what are you going to do about it?" she asked.

"Nothing," replied Stormleaper bluntly, "because Winterwarrior made me promise not to break our bond."

"Is that so," said the young Britania, raising her eyebrows and pursing her lips together.

Then Stormleaper bid Britania good evening as he continued his walk deep in thought and she remained talking to her warriors.

The feasting went on long into the night as strong drink was set up with choicest meats and fish and varied fruits. Courage and calmness rose up within the fighting men as the feast was misted over with mindmadness and a haze of dim delusion shadowed the singers. The malice-talk and the word-wounding did not end until the sunrise dawned on another day.

The next morning the Hawkarmy performed their display before the crowd and then everyone returned to the main hall.

When Summersailor saw Stormleaper returning to the hall he spoke to him hoping to avoid any more trouble and maintain the peace.   So he whispered to the grim Stormleaper, "Have you still made up your mind to keep your calm?"

"I will not lay a hand nor even touch him," answered the Stormleaper.

Then Summersailor nodded and went his way but watched.

Flyingbat stretched and sneered and shouted at Stormleaper who was standing nearby, "Ah, here is the man whose own father was killed by my brother Oakhill.

"That exhibition of the Hawkarmy was surely a work of battleart designed to scare us.   All that display of sham-fight would have been well named for what it was just phony show-off."

But Stormleaper was determined not to be provoked and Winterwarrior also kept a watchful eye on him as Flyingbat continued his tirade.

"If my brother Oakhill had been here he would have challenged each one of them to single combat and defeated them and destroyed them, one by one and thrown their drained-out bodies into a pit of wolves to eat for breakfast.

"If only my fierce brother had been here. He is a tormentor whom all men fear, yes, even I his young brother."

As his boasting continued, among those who also rejoined all the guests inside the castle was the WarQueen Britania who came back followed by two humble servants carrying wooden boxes.

Although the sun had shone for the display, the long clouds gathered in the sky as the young WarQueen Britania grimly strode up to the feasting. It seemed like a shadow fell on the assembly just like the black smoke pall that drapes a palace when a king draws near to it on a winter's night.

A silence fell on many who watched her and the servants walking purposefully towards Flyingbat. The crowd stood frozen and puzzled as they wondered what was this all about.

The witches paused with slanty eyes of insight, suspicion and fear and began to whisper and point as the servants shuddered and stumbled. One of the servants appeared to splutter and to cough and groan.

Then Britania spoke directly to the boastful Flyingbat, "Flyingbat, then tremble in good faith for he is here," cried the young Britania, "Oakhill has arrived. He walks beside me. I have brought him here, fresh from the bloodbath combat, to greet his younger brother."

Then she bowed and waved her hand respectfully towards the servants. Flyingbat laughed but others froze in silence, hearing strange sounds and seeing some drops of blood.

Others moved away, shuddering as Flyingbat sneered, "This foolish woman thinks that I do not recognize my brother. I have never even seen this servingman before."

"Permit me, Flyingbat," responded Britania.

And suddenly she seized the head of Oakhill out of the box, held by the trusty servant, shaking the head by the hair into the face of Flyingbat.

"See, boaster - here is your fierce brother. Recognize him now? Oakhill has just been slain in fatal combat."

Men gasped and shuddered in silence as Britania shook out the still-live head of Oakhill, grizzled with pain, snarled up with the grimacing torture of dread death. She threw the head upon the table of Flyingbat.

As the head rolled down onto the table it groaned and spat and splattered blood on the younger brother.

The head screamed, "Kill me my brother and save me from this pain."

Then it opened its mouth and stared and died. And blood rose up out of the mouth of Flyingbat and then he fell dead on the head of his fierce brother.

Then Britania beckoned to the other servants to come forward and open their box.

"And here are those to paid your brother for his brutal murders," cried Britania.

Out of the boxes fell the heads of King Warchariot and his WarQueen Snakeknife.

The witch Landslink rose up and screamed, "You have broken bond."

But Whaleroarer cried out, "No, this was fair. Oakhill was never here. He was killed far from the castle, outside the bond and promise of our agreement. It is just like the murder of my good old dog, Guardhunt. As for the king and queen, I know not nor care not how they met their fate."

Britania shouted out for all to hear, "WarQueen Snakeknife told Oakhill to murder fieldmarshal Winterwarrior. He refused because he had heard that Winterwarrior was to be the next king. They fought and killed each other. But it was I, the daughter of King Waterbear, who murdered Warchariot. You all know why."

Windweasel cried, "Dogs, dogs! No! This is war. The time for talking of peace is dead and gone."

And Meteoreyes cried out, "So you want war. Let war be war and choose whom you will serve."

And the servant of Flyingbat quietly handed the Bonespear to the Stormleaper and no one dared to query that the Stormleaper was the winner who had earned the deadly Bonespear.

The Shield of Roar was placed beside Winterwarrior.

Then WarQueen Britania laughed, speaking to her three ladies, "As if those hags had ever any intention of speaking peace. What fools men are! Yes, let all men choose well, whether to fight for good or ill, to waiver or to remain loyal to Truthteller."

But Winterwarrior, the veteran fieldmarshal of the Eagles shouted out, "Stop this madness now. There will be no more fighting and no more wars. Enough is enough."

His deputy Summersailor shouted out, "Wars are the last thing we all want or need."

Winterwarrior spoke directly to the four witches, "Your time for evil is finished now that your masters King Warchariot and his evil WarQueen Snakeknife are no more. For no one in this assembly will be consulting with you."

So the four witches slunk away through the back entrances of the castle as the entire assembly of Eagle Warriors were loudly cheering and shouting for Winterwarrior, as they proclaimed him as the King of the Eagle Warriors.

Then Winterwarrior, the new King of the Eagles, addressed Summersailor, "Stay with me for a while as my fieldmarshal to help me gather together my new and friendly kingdom."

Summersailor smiled and nodded in agreement but assured Britania, "I will rejoin the Wavewarriors again one day soon."

Later, when WarQueen Britania left the castle with her followers, she stopped her chariot for a moment to salute King Winterwarrior, the new King of the Eagles and fieldmarshal Summersailor.

Then one of the Eagle Warriors waved the Rainbowsword and the rainbow flew in a straight line down the middle of the army. The Hawk Warriors drew their chariots back, to leave a pathway cleared for the Wavewarriors who were followed by their WarQueen Britania and her three fieldmarshals – Icedragon, Stormleaper and Whaleroarer with their warqueens. And finally the Hawkarmy pride of the Seagulls at the rear of the procession.

Meanwhile, alone in the great hall, the heads of Warchariot, Snakeknife and Oakhill lay cold and deserted. Three heads and a body on the table of fruit and bread and wine where the corpse of Flyingbat, the proud and boastful younger brother, lay frozen as the winds of peace began to slowly blow through the corridors of the castle.

*****

GHOSTS OF THE WHITE AND THE BAY

The Great Bay Stallion of the West, Foresthorse, came to meet the Great White Stallion of the East, Oceanhorse. The White roared up and reared and kicked his hooves. The White snorted and looked over all his herds so the Bay calmed down and did not make a challenge. The Bay realized that the war was lost and won so he drew back and galloped off to find the wild herds that rambled loose upon the moors.

So the Great Bay and the Great White led their herds separately and on peaceful plains to gallop in the warm air with honeybees and bushes and cool springs flowing through the shaded trees.

Even today they gallop in the night and on the Bay's broad back there sits Winterwarrior and on the Great White Stallion sits Britania, the ghosts of warriors past and gone and lost.

Now they are no longer troubled with the ways of war - the first thing to prepare for but the last thing that you need in this short life for there is no such thing as a won war.

Only Weather wins. Water and fire and wind and the earth plates and the grey buzzards triumph at the end as the elements sweep over the derelict camps of troops and horses.

The Great White and the Great Bay still gallop as they once did in the early days of war when they were ridden by Waterbear and the Warchariot. But now they are dark in the moonlight, grim even in shadows.

The End